LOOK AT ALL THOSE ROSES

'TEARS, IDLE TEARS'

ELIZABETH BOWEN

LOOK AT ALL THOSE ROSES

ROSES

Short Stories

JONATHAN CAPE
THIRTY BEDFORD SQUARE
LONDON

FIRST PUBLISHED 1941
FIRST PUBLISHED IN THE COLLECTED EDITION 1951

PRINTED IN GREAT BRITAIN IN THE CITY OF OXFORD
AT THE ALDEN PRESS
BOUND BY A. W. BAIN & CO. LTD., LONDON

LOOK AT ALL THOSE ROSES

10-28-57- B. H. Blackwell - #1. 5s

CONTENTS

REDUCED

THE Carburys' two little girls, Penny and Claudia, went upstairs again with their governess, Miss Rice, as soon as lunch was over; their steps could be heard retreating along the pitch-pine gallery round the hall. The visitors were disappointed – Mrs. Laurie liked children and Frank Peele had been hoping to see more of the governess. Rain drummed on the hall skylight; still smoking their host Godwin Carbury's rather musty cigarettes, the grown-ups allowed themselves to be driven into the library. Here no chair invited you, the uninviting books must have been bought in lots, and looked gummed in the shelves. It could have been a pretty September day; the plum-tree leaves in the tilting orchards round were bright yellow, but for days the Forest of Dene had been clouded and sodden.

Mrs. Laurie, who was vivacious and had married at nineteen, and Mrs. Carbury, who was muddled and dim, had been friends years ago in India when they were both young girls. They had kept in touch, Mrs. Carbury having no other vivacious friend, life having taught Mrs. Laurie that there was no knowing when anybody devoted might not come in useful – besides, she had always been sorry for Mima.

Mima's life had been unrewarding. She returned

flatly from India after her friend's wedding, and it had not been till she was twenty-seven or eight that she met Godwin Carbury, who at forty was looking round for a wife. He had the reputation of being the most unpopular man in his part of the country, and that reputation followed him up to London. He was careful, savagely careful, about money and not careful enough about seeing this was not known. Added to this, he had a dour self-importance. It was understood that economy kept him single as long as his mother had lived to keep house at Pendlethwaite. Possibly Mima saw something in him that no one else saw; she was anxious to 'settle' suitably, and not herself accustomed to being liked. At all events, they married, and had had after some years these two thin, remote little girls. They had few neighbours at Pendlethwaite and Godwin's peculiarities cut them off more and more from anybody there was. Whatever misgivings she had, Mima pandered to him blindly. On her own account she had just a little money, so once or twice a year she came up to London, gazed into shop windows, met Mrs. Laurie (now widowed) and bought reduced coats and shoes for the little girls. She had begun lately to talk of giving up London; the girls' education would be a heavy expense, she said.

It surprised Mrs. Laurie to find herself at Pendle-thwaite, but she had been at a loose end, with nowhere to go for a week. So she thought, 'Try the Carburys', and had written to Mima. She was a shiftless woman, maintaining herself by the exercise of a good deal of charm: she could say daring things without sounding impertinent, and determined to get a little fun out of Godwin – apart from this, she did not expect very much.

Pendlethwaite was not a lovable house. Built about

1880 of unpleasing maroon brick, it creaked inside with pitch-pine; its church-like windows peered narrowly at the smiling landscape round; its grounds darkened a valley with belts of laurel and stiff, damp-looking clumps of unindigenous firs. The house looked dedicated to a perpetual January: sunnier seasons beat back from its walls. The bloomy red plums and mellow apples bending the boughs this month were pagan company for it. Indoors, there was no electricity; panels absorbed the lamplight; before October, no fires were lit till night. It had not even the insidious charm of decay, for Godwin had great ideas of keeping things up: the laurels were kept clipped, the thrifty meals served formally . . . Mrs. Laurie had been diverted to find that she had a fellow guest, but this did not see her far. Frank Peele, just back on leave from Siam, was Mima's second cousin. He must have asked himself here because he had to be somewhere; she thought he was not a man you would scramble to entertain. At about thirty, he was a haggard schoolboy — shambling, facetious, huffy, forlorn, melancholic, with perhaps (she feared most of all) a romantic soul. She supposed Mima must enjoy being even sorrier for him than she need be for herself . . . Entertaining on this scale must be a plunge for the Carburys. Mrs. Laurie could almost hear Godwin saying to Mima: 'Well then, in for a penny, in for a pound.' He went through with his duties as host with glum correctness. 'But if one stayed a day too long he'd cut off supplies.' As it was, his rigid economies hit you everywhere.

The one startling un-economy was the governess. Mrs. Laurie, though unhappily childless, knew an expensive governess when she saw one. Miss Rice's technique was perfect. Her first appearance, at lunch, took Nella's breath away with its unobtrusiveness. Penny and Claudia – their dark eyes set close in, tucking their long, fair hair back behind their shoulders primly – clearly revolved round her. 'Those two little mice adore her,' thought Mrs. Laurie, recalling the composed retreat after lunch: three people going back to a world of their own. But the adoration was kept within nice bounds. 'How does Mima *keep* the woman in this mausoleum? She might be anywhere. Mima can't be such a fool as I thought . . . I must find out.'

In the library, she lost no time in doing this. In the bow window, Frank Peele with his hands in his pockets stood looking out unexpectantly at the rain; Mima poured out thin coffee; Godwin glumly handed the cups round. Mrs. Laurie said affably: 'So you got a governess? Last time we met, you were busy looking for one.'

'Yes, oh yes. We did,' Mima said in her flustered way.

'Miss Rice came in May,' said Godwin firmly.

'She seems a great success. . . .'

Frank Peele grunted.

'When she first came in,' went on Mrs. Laurie, 'I felt certain I'd seen her somewhere. I wonder where she was before? She's startlingly good-looking, but in such a tactful way. Hag-ridden – but that's the life, I suppose.'

'She appears content with us,' said Godwin, handing the sugar to Mrs. Laurie bitterly. 'Mima, what are your plans for this afternoon?' His wife looked blank.

'Our guests should be entertained.'

'It struck me,' said Frank, wheeling round, 'as one of the few faces I had not seen before.'

'Really?' said Godwin.

Mima touched the coffee-tray clumsily; everything on it skidded. Did she not want Cousin Frank to fall for the governess? The nicest women like having unattached men around. 'She must be full of brains,' said Mrs. Laurie vaguely.

'She teaches wonderfully; she's got the children on so. They seem to be learning everything.'

'Can we have them all down after tea to play Up Jenkin or something?'

'They do preparation then,' said Godwin repressively. ('Set,' thought his guest, 'on getting his money's worth.') Mima's eyes, oddly overwrought in her pink, creased face, stole to meet her husband's. 'Frank,' Godwin continued, 'I could show you those maps now.' Clearly, any discussion of Miss Rice was closed.

'Not today, thanks,' said Frank, 'I've got a crick in my neck.' Godwin, after one more forbidding look at Mima, left them, shutting the door reprovingly. Frank loafed along the bookshelves, pulled out *Monasteries of the Levant*, and folded himself in a chair with an air of resigned discomfort. A man with a book is practically not present. Mrs. Laurie whipped out her *petit point*, and the two women, pulling their chairs together zestfully, settled down for a talk. Rain streamed down the windows, paper rustled inside the cold grate.

Mima saw so few friends that talk went to her head like wine. Evenly sing-song, the women's voices began rising and falling. After half an hour, Frank's book slipped on to his knee; his head rolled back, jaw dropping; he let out a sharp snore. 'Really . . .' exclaimed Mima, stopping the talk to titter. 'A tropical habit,' said Mrs. Laurie. This was better than Frank with a book, they were quite alone. She hopped back to her topic.

'Mima, what's Godwin got up his sleeve about Miss Rice?'

'Miss Rice? – nothing,' Mima said, over-acting.

'His one wicked extravagance?'

'No,' faltered Mima. 'That's just the point – she's not.'

'A bargain? You amaze me. Can she be at all fishy?'

'My dear Nella – she's good with the children, isn't she?' Mima fixed her friend with such oddly imploring eyes that Mrs. Laurie, startled, put down her work: 'She's made princesses of them,' she said extravagantly. 'How wise you have been, Mima!'

'You do really think so? Godwin and I wanted the best we could get, you see: he has such ideas for Penny and Claudia.'

'It does him credit,' said Mrs. Laurie warmly.

'I suppose so——' blurted out Mima – then, looking wretched, put her hand to her cheek. 'I've never quite liked – I mean if she – I can't help wondering——'

'Why did Godwin snap me up when I said I thought I knew her face?'

'We'd hoped no one would think that,' said Mima surprisingly. 'As a rule, you see, almost nobody comes here, and in every other way she seemed quite ideal: she is. In the ordinary way, we never could have afforded her. It did seem such an opportunity. You see, we could not offer a high salary.'

'That would narrow things down. . . .'

'It did. All the ones I had interviewed were so vulgar and pushing, besides seeming to know nothing at all. The agency woman said, "For that, what can you expect?" I was in despair.'

'Oh? So then——?'

'I came round more and more to Godwin's idea. As he said, it was practically a charity. It did seem unfair that

16

the thing should count against her. When she had paid
for her defence she hadn't a penny, and no other future,
of course. And she was acquitted.'

'What on earth do you mean?'

Looking thoroughly frightened, Mima caught herself
up. 'Oh dear,' she said, 'and I swore never to speak of it.
Nella, will you swear to let this go no further? It's such
a relief to tell you: it's on my mind the whole time. You
see, Godwin had followed all the evidence carefully.
The witnesses gave her such magnificent testimonials,
almost all her former employers were called. Even the
Prosecution didn't make out she wasn't a good *governess*.
And after all, she was cleared. (If only they'd found
who'd done it. . . .)'

'Begin at the beginning.'

'Well . . . Do you ever read murder trials?'

'Hardly ever miss one.'

'Do you remember that Sir Max Rant dying suddenly?'

'Mima – she's not *Henrietta Post*?'

'Sssh – sssh,' whispered Mima, glancing Frank's way
cautiously. Then she nodded at Nella with frightened,
important eyes.

Mrs. Laurie stared, galvanized, at her hostess. Then:
'She's lucky to be alive,' she said. 'It was touch and go.'

'He was a dreadful old man, apparently. At the very
worst, they said nothing against her *morals*.'

'No wonder she's haunted-looking. That was an
appalling ordeal . . . But, after that, how on earth——?'

'Godwin got me to write to her three weeks after the
trial, offering her a new life and twenty-five pounds a
year. . . .'

'Godwin is on the spot! Well, they're your children,
not mine – *Henrietta Post!*'

Immovably, without batting a closed eyelid, Frank said, 'Who is Henrietta Post?'

II

'Miss Rice's hands are cold again,' said Penny.

Claudia went on painting a moment longer, then, balancing her brush on the glass jar of paint-water, which gave out a prussic smell and had a red sediment, looked intently across the table at Penny, who stood by Miss Rice's chair, chafing her right hand. Their governess, with her book propped on the table, her pale cheek on her left hand, read on, smiling unnoticingly. Once she withdrew her hand from Penny's to turn over a page.

'Whatever will she do in winter?' said Claudia.

'There'll be fires then.'

'This fire never burns much.' They shared the same desperate thought: 'Suppose our darling should leave us?'

This afternoon, the black chill of the grate focused your fancy as firelight might have done. The schoolroom had a faded sea-blue wallpaper cut into by pitchpine presses and two doors: not a colour warmed it; the high windows looked into a rain-blurred hill. Miss Rice had put nothing of her own on the mantelpiece, along which marched a file of plasticine animals modelled by the little girls. About the room were products of other hobbies good governesses encourage children to have – on the windowsill a nursery-garden in pots: pink-cheeked 'Bubbles' and 'Cherry Ripe' looked queerly down at the bleak room where these three people were living as best they could.

Miss Rice put away the book and with it her happy, forgetful smile – the book had been *Emma*. 'Have you stopped painting?' she said.

She had given them for their subject a Greek temple. Claudia's temple had a sunset behind it, Penny had filled in the columns with Mediterranean blue. Miss Rice came round and looked. 'A sunset like that would make reflections on white stone, Claudia. Penny, on such a fine day there would be shadows.' They saw. She always thought of something they had not thought of: they wrinkled up their foreheads in ecstatic despair. 'Penny, if you are stopping, wash that blue off your paint-brush.'

'Are paints poison?'

'Sometimes. Well, are you cold, too?'

They would admit nothing that could distress her.

'Then push the table back and get the skipping-ropes out.'

The little girls were alike, though there were two years between them, as though they could not decide to part in any particular. There was not much difference in size, as though Penny had waited for Claudia. Their voices were pitched on the same persuasive note; when their vehement dark eyes met they seemed to consult. What they thought of being alive their parents would never know; their characters were like batteries storing something up. Before Miss Rice was here, the doctor's sister had come in every morning to give them lessons. They had known before how to read and write, so all they had learnt from the doctor's sister was what every-one else knew: just why their house was avoided, how bitterly father was laughed at and mother pitied because of him. They learnt that it was wretched to be them-selves. They marked the contempt with which every morning she bicycled up their avenue, and how insolently she ate what there was at lunch. Her raspy finger-tips, the pearls screwed tight in her fleshy ears, her horse-sense, all seemed part of her power to mortify them. She was the world and they prayed she might die, but she married. After that they waited, in armour. Then came Miss Rice.

'If you want to keep warm you must hurry,' said Miss Rice.

Claudia unwound the skipping-ropes and they took one each: they stood with their arms out, gripping the handles eagerly. 'One, two, three – go!' The ropes zip-zipped on the oilcloth. Penny stumbled at fifty-six, but Claudia kept in and skipped seventy-eight: her toes bounced and bounced, her hair flopped, her eyes started out of her head. At last the rope caught her toe. 'That's the record,' said Miss Rice, 'but Penny may beat it next time.' Both breathless they knelt on the hearthrug, life tingling up through them from their toes to their cheeks.

'If you skipped,' said Claudia, 'you might skip a hundred.'

'The rope is too short,' said Miss Rice.

'What else used you to do – dance?'

'Yes, once.'

They had never seen anyone dancing except in pictures of ballrooms; they preferred to imagine Miss Rice not on the crook of an arm but floating alone around a floor, with her ageless, shining white face, unfrivolous as an angel. At this happy moment, near her and warm from skipping, they felt on the edge of the story she did not tell . . . But *she* looked down at the skipping-ropes on the floor. 'Better put those away,' she said. Except when she was reading she never stayed quiet long: something they could feel creep up behind her chair would make her speaking eyes go suddenly cold and dark as the grate. Against this their love was powerless. This dreadful expectation seemed wrong in their darling – mother without her worries would not be anyone, father was there to stare and bite his moustache, but she seemed to them born to inherit light . . . Feeling their enemy here now the children, helpless, got up to put the skipping-ropes back in the press.

'Someone's coming!' said Penny. They heard the baize door at the far end of their passage swing to behind somebody, then a man's step. A knuckle rapped the door once, unconfidently: Miss Rice and the children waited. 'Come in,' she said.

Franke Peele peered round the door. 'Oh?' he said. 'May I come in? Sorry, I was exploring. Looking for secret passages. Exercise before tea.' Miss Rice smiled composedly. 'So here you all are,' he went on. He looked at the table. 'Painting?'

'Yes.'

'What a day!' he said to Miss Rice humbly. 'Very cheery up here, though. You believe in fresh air?' Then he saw that both windows were bolted: what he felt were the draughts. Miss Rice had moved to the table where she had been reading; Frank dropped into the wicker chair with a creak. The children shut their paint-boxes up. 'Must be getting on tea time,' remarked Frank.

'Are you hungry, Cousin Frank?' said Claudia gently.

Frank looked relieved at hearing someone say something. 'I don't deserve tea; I slept like a log in the library. Your mother and Mrs. Laurie complain I snored.' He looked round the schoolroom wistfully, like a dog. 'They were talking nineteen to the dozen. When I dropped off they were well away about India; when I came to it was one Henrietta Post.'

Penny laughed. 'Who's Henrietta Post?' she said.

'Don't ask me,' said Frank. 'Miss Rice, who's Henrietta Post?'

Miss Rice pondered while the clock ticked several seconds and a cart rattled off into silence behind the wet orchards. The children turned to see how she took Frank's joke. She looked twice at him with steady, considering dark eyes. 'Surely you know?' she said at last.

'I don't know a soul,' said Frank, 'I've been in Siam.'

'But you get the papers there, don't you?'

'She's a celebrity, is she?'

'She was accused of murder,' said Miss Rice, as though giving a history lesson, 'tried last spring, acquitted, but never properly cleared. So she disappeared, hoping to be forgotten.'

'Good God,' exclaimed Frank. 'Where would a woman go to, after a show like that?'

'She is fortunate to be anywhere.'

'Stop: it's coming back!' Frank said, delighted to have a topic. 'Wasn't she that governess? The old swine whose house she was in had been making up to her, so when someone did him in they tried to fix it on her. I remember I thought at the time——'

Miss Rice's marked unresponse reminded Frank where he was. Chidden, he stopped awkwardly, with a glance at the children. *They* sat stone-still, clasped hands thrust down between their knees; you could not possibly tell what was going on in their heads, which were both turned intently away from their governess. Frank kicked himself. But for the life of him he couldn't stop blurting out: 'She was very good-looking, wasn't she?'

'You never saw any photographs?'

'Out where I am I only get *The Times*, you see. No pretty pictures in it.'

'I see.'

Frank went on violently: 'I know I thought at the time what a shocking, unfair thing to happen to any woman!' . . . Miss Rice with her cold smile looked thoughtfully into the grate as though there were a fire burning there: she said nothing more. Her charges' agonized tension became startling. Frank hummed and beat a nonplussed tattoo on his knee. They were waiting to see the last of him. Whatever brick one had dropped, they were all very odd up here. . . .

This wet autumn evening closed in so early that the children had to stop work and wait for the lamp to come; when Mrs. Carbury looked in they were all in the dark. 'Why, whatever are you doing?' she said nervously. 'Where's Miss Rice? Why doesn't she ring for the lamp?'

'It never comes any sooner.'

'Father wouldn't like you wasting your time like this. Where is Miss Rice?'

'In her room,' Penny said, so indifferently that there seemed to be something foolish about the fuss. At this point a band of light appeared in the passage; the housemaid brought in the lamp and Mima saw her daughters facing each other like images across the table of lesson books, their unchildish eyes dark in the sudden lamplight. She sat down, acting calm while the housemaid was in the room; all the same, her manner made the girl so jumpy that she went away again without drawing down the blinds. Mrs. Carbury sat eyeing the other door; the children's bedroom opened off the schoolroom and Miss Rice's room was beyond, connecting with theirs. Her relief at not finding the governess was tremendous: all the same, she felt she was being defied.

'Does she always leave you to do preparation alone?'

'She's tired,' said Claudia. 'Cousin Frank was up here.'

'Oh? . . . Well, tell her I want to speak to her. Then you can leave your lessons, just for this evening, and go downstairs; Mrs. Laurie says she will play games with you.'

The children looked at their books without stirring, and Mima for the first time felt mutiny in the air . . . Mima had had to brace herself to come in; twice already since tea she had started up to the schoolroom, then turned back before the baize door to that wing. Ever since her revelation to Mrs. Laurie she had been in a fearful state: the way Mrs. Laurie took it brought her own most persistent throttling fears to the top: 'Henrietta Post . . . Well, they're your children, not mine.' What Nella said was what anybody who knew would say. Mima had shrunk back from the schoolroom door, feeling: 'No, I really cannot face her.' Then she had been forced to think: 'But that is the woman my children are with the whole time . . .' Once she had gone as far as Godwin's study to tell him he must agree to send Miss Rice away tomorrow, but the way he had looked up at her settled that. 'Nothing has changed since I agreed to engage her.' Mima knew too well that her husband found her a fool. 'I will give her notice first, then tell Godwin. It won't be so bad with Nella in the house here. Nella will back me up. *But when Godwin hears I've told Nella?* . . . He said before she came to stay: "Suppose your friend is inquisitive?" . . . What are they doing up there?

What does she say to them? What goes on the whole time? My own children are strangers; they don't like being downstairs now. *What was it the prosecution said about influence?*'

Mima raised her voice. 'Run along now at once, children: Mrs. Laurie is waiting.'

'We would much rather not, mother.'

'Then you're very ungrateful. Besides, I have got something to say to Miss Rice – Penny and Claudia, don't look at each other like that! It's rude to look at each other when mother speaks!'

'Miss Rice is tired,' repeated Claudia gently.

'If you give us the message,' said Penny, 'we'll tell her.'

'No, I want to talk to Miss Rice,' said Mima, her voice unnatural.

'Do you, mother?' said Penny. 'You don't generally.'

The wicker chair Mima sat in creaked convulsively. 'When we're alone again you may learn to make your mother happy. You may understand mother then and not be unkind to her. Tomorrow, Miss Rice will be going away, children.'

Penny and Claudia looked at the chair their mother now sat in, then up at *Emma* left on the edge of the mantelpiece. Claudia looked at their row of young plants in the windowsill, sharp in the lamplight against the rain-lashed dark outside, Penny at the wrinkled rug where that afternoon they had knelt at their darling's feet. Then their gentle, vehement dark eyes, meeting, paused to consult again. They said in their quiet voices: 'Then we will go too.'

TEARS, IDLE TEARS

FREDERICK burst into tears in the middle of Regent's Park. His mother, seeing what was about to happen, had cried: 'Frederick, you *can't* – in the middle of Regent's Park!' Really, this was a corner, one of those lively corners just inside a big gate, where two walks meet and a bridge starts across the pretty, winding lake. People were passing quickly; the bridge rang with feet. Poplars stood up like delicate green brooms; diaphanous willows whose weeping was not shocking quivered over the lake. May sun spattered gold through the breezy trees; the tulips though falling open were still gay; three girls in a long boat shot under the bridge. Frederick, knees trembling, butted towards his mother a crimson, convulsed face, as though he had the idea of burying himself in her. She whipped out a handkerchief and dabbed at him with it under his grey felt hat, exclaiming meanwhile in fearful mortification: 'You really haven't got to be such a *baby*!' Her tone attracted the notice of several people, who might otherwise have thought he was having something taken out of his eye.

He was too big to cry: the whole scene was disgraceful. He wore a grey flannel knickerbocker suit and looked like a schoolboy; though in fact he was seven, still doing lessons at home. His mother said to him almost every week: 'I don't know what they will think when you go to school!' His tears were a shame of which she could speak to no one; no offensive weakness of body could have upset her more. Once she had got so far as taking her pen up to write to the Mother's Advice Column of a helpful woman's weekly about them. She began: 'I am a widow; young, good tempered, and my friends all tell me that I have great control. But my little boy——' She intended to sign herself 'Mrs. D., Surrey.' But then she had stopped and thought no, no: after all, he is Toppy's son . . . She was a gallant-looking, correct woman, wearing today in London a coat and skirt, a silver fox, white gloves and a dark-blue toque put on exactly right – not the sort of woman you ought to see in a Park with a great blubbering boy belonging to her. She looked a mother of sons, but not of a son of this kind, and should more properly, really, have been walking a dog. 'Come on!' she said, as though the bridge, the poplars, the people staring were to be borne no longer. She began to walk on quickly, along the edge of the lake, parallel with the park's girdle of trees and the dark, haughty windows of Cornwall Terrace looking at her over the red may. They had meant to go to the Zoo, but now she had changed her mind: Frederick did not deserve the Zoo.

Frederick stumbled along beside her, too miserable to notice. His mother seldom openly punished him, but often revenged herself on him in small ways. He could feel how just this was. His own incontinence in the matter of tears was as shocking to him, as bowing-down, as annulling, as it could be to her. He never knew what happened – a cold, black pit with no bottom opened inside himself; a red-hot bellwire jagged up through him from the pit of his frozen belly to the caves of his eyes. Then the hot, gummy rush of tears, the convulsion of his features, the terrible, square grin he felt his mouth take all made him his own shameful and squalid enemy. Despair howled round his inside like a wind, and through his streaming eyes he saw everything quake. Anyone's being there – and most of all his mother – drove this catastrophe on him. He never cried like this when he was alone.

Crying made him so abject, so outcast from other people that he went on crying out of despair. His crying was not just reflex, like a baby's; it dragged up all unseemliness into view. No wonder everyone was repelled. There is something about an abject person that rouses cruelty in the kindest breast. The plate-glass windows of the lordly houses looked at him through the may-trees with judges' eyes. Girls with their knees crossed, reading on the park benches, looked up with unkind smiles. His apathetic stumbling, his not seeing or caring that they had given up their trip to the Zoo, became more than Mrs. Dickinson, his mother, could bear. She pointed out, in a voice tense with dislike: 'I'm not taking you to the Zoo.'

'Mmmph-mmph-mmph,' sobbed Frederick.

'You know, I so often wonder what your father would think.'

'Mmmph-mmph-mmph.'

'He used to be so proud of you. He and I used to look forward to what you'd be like when you were a big boy. One of the last things he ever said was: "Frederick will take care of you." You almost make me glad he's not here now.'

'Oough-oough.'

'What do you say?'

'I'm t-t-trying to stop.'

'Everybody's looking at you, you know.'

She was one of those women who have an unfailing sense of what not to say, and say it: despair, perversity or stubborn virtue must actuate them. She had a horror, also, of the abnormal and had to hit out at it before it could hit at her. Her husband, an R.A.F. pilot who had died two days after a ghastly crash, after two or three harrowing spaces of consciousness, had never made her ashamed or puzzled her. Their intimacies, then even his death, had had a bold naturalness.

'Listen, I shall walk on ahead,' said Frederick's mother, lifting her chin with that noble, decided movement so many people liked. 'You stay here and look at that duck till you've stopped that noise. Don't catch me up till you have. No, I'm really ashamed of you.'

She walked on. He had *not* been making, really, so very much noise. Drawing choppy breaths, he stood still and looked at the duck that sat folded into a sleek white cypher on the green, grassy margin of the lake. When it rolled one eye open over a curve, something unseeing in its expression calmed him. His mother walked away under the gay tree-shadows; her step quickened lightly, the tip of her fox fur swung. She thought of the lunch she had had with Major and Mrs. Williams, the party she would be going to at five. First, she must leave Frederick at Aunt Mary's, and what would Aunt Mary say to his bloated face? She walked fast; the gap between her and Frederick widened: she was a charming woman walking by herself.

Everybody had noticed how much courage she had; they said: 'How plucky Mrs. Dickinson is.' It was five years since her tragedy and she had not remarried, so

that her gallantness kept on coming into play. She helped
a friend with a little hat shop called *Isobel* near where
they lived in Surrey, bred puppies for sale and gave the
rest of her time to making a man of Frederick. She
smiled nicely and carried her head high. Those two days
while Toppy had lain dying she had hardly turned a
hair, for his sake: no one knew when he might come
conscious again. When she was not by his bed she was
waiting about the hospital. The chaplain hanging about
her and the doctor had given thanks that there were
women like this; another officer's wife who had been her
friend had said she was braver than could be good for
anyone. When Toppy finally died the other woman had
put the unflinching widow into a taxi and driven back
with her to the Dickinsons' bungalow. She kept saying:
'Cry, dear, cry: you'd feel better.' She made tea and
clattered about, repeating: 'Don't mind me, darling:
just have a big cry.' The strain became so great that
tears streamed down her own face. Mrs. Dickinson
looked past her palely, with a polite smile. The empty-
feeling bungalow with its rustling curtains still smelt of
Toppy's pipe; his slippers were under a chair. Then
Mrs. Dickinson's friend, almost tittering with despair,
thought of a poem of Tennyson's she had learnt as a
child. She said: 'Where's Frederick? He's quiet. Do
you think he's asleep?' The widow, rising, perfectly
automatic, led her into the room where Frederick lay in
his cot. A nursemaid rose from beside him, gave them
one morbid look and scurried away. The two-year-old
baby, flushed, and drawing up his upper lip in his sleep
as his father used to do, lay curved under his blue blanket,
clenching one fist on nothing. Something suddenly
seemed to strike his mother, who, slumping down by

the cot, ground her face and forehead into the fluffy blanket, then began winding the blanket round her two fists. Her convulsions, though proper, were fearful: the cot shook. The friend crept away into the kitchen, where she stayed a half-hour, muttering to the maid. They made more tea and waited for Mrs. Dickinson to give full birth to her grief. Then extreme silence drew them back to the cot. Mrs. Dickinson knelt asleep, her profile pressed to the blanket, one arm crooked over the baby's form. Under his mother's arm, as still as an image, Frederick lay wide awake, not making a sound. In conjunction with a certain look in his eyes, the baby's silence gave the two women the horrors. The servant said to the friend: 'You would think he knew.'

Mrs. Dickinson's making so few demands on pity soon rather alienated her women friends, but men liked her better for it: several of them found in her straight look an involuntary appeal to themselves alone, more exciting than coquetry, deeply, nobly exciting: several wanted to marry her. But courage had given her a new intractable kind of virgin pride: she loved it too much; she could never surrender it. 'No, don't ask me that,' she would say, lifting her chin and with that calm, gallant smile. 'Don't spoil things. You've been splendid to me: such a support. But you see, there's Frederick. He's the man in my life now. I'm bound to put him first. That wouldn't be fair, would it?' After that, she would simply go on shaking her head. She became the perfect friend for men who wished to wish to marry but were just as glad not to, and for married men who liked just a little pathos without being upset.

Frederick had stopped crying. This left him perfectly blank, so that he stared at the duck with abstract intensity, perceiving its moulded feathers and porcelain-smooth neck. The burning, swirling film had cleared away from his eyes, and his diaphragm felt relief, as when retching has stopped. He forgot his focus of grief and forgot his mother, but saw with joy a quivering bough of willow that, drooping into his gaze under his swollen eyelids, looked as pure and strong as something after the Flood. His thought clutched at the willow, weak and wrecked but happy. He knew he was now qualified to walk after his mother, but without feeling either guilty or recalcitrant did not wish to do so. He stepped over the rail – no park keeper being at hand to stop him – and, tenderly and respectfully, attempted to touch the white duck's tail. Without a blink, with automatic uncoyness, the duck slid away from Frederick into the lake. Its lovely white-china body balanced on the green glass water as it propelled itself gently round the curve of the bank. Frederick saw with a passion of observation its shadowy, webbed feet lazily striking out.

'The keeper'll eat you,' said a voice behind him.

Frederick looked cautiously round with his bunged-up eyes. The *individual* who had spoken sat on a park bench; it was a girl with a dispatch case beside her. Her big bony knee-joints stuck out through her thin crêpe-de-chine dress; she was hatless and her hair made a frizzy, pretty outline, but she wore spectacles, her skin had burnt dull red; her smile and the cock of her head had about them something pungent and energetic, not like a girl's at all. 'Whatcher mean, eat me?'

'You're on his grass. And putting salt on his duck's tail.'

Frederick stepped back carefully over the low rail.

'I haven't got any salt.' He looked up and down the walk: his mother was out of sight, but from the direction of the bridge a keeper was approaching, still distant but with an awesome gait. 'My goodness,' the girl said, 'what's been biting *you*?' Frederick was at a loss. 'Here,' she said, 'have an apple.' She opened her case, which was full of folded grease-paper that must have held sandwiches, and rummaged out an apple with a waxy, bright skin. Frederick came up, tentative as a pony, and finally took the apple. His breath was still hitching and catching; he did not wish to speak.

'Go on,' she said, 'swallow: it'll settle your chest. Where's your mother gone off to? What's all the noise about?' Frederick only opened his jaws as wide as they would go, then bit slowly, deeply into the apple. The girl re-crossed her legs and tucked her thin crêpe-de-chine skirt round the other knee. 'What had you done — cheeked her?'

Frederick swept the mouthful of apple into one cheek. 'No,' he said shortly. 'Cried.'

'I should say you did. Bellowed, I watched you all down the path.' There was something ruminative in the girl's tone that made her remark really not at all offensive; in fact, she looked at Frederick as though she were meeting an artist who had just done a turn. He had been standing about, licking and biting the apple, but now he came and sat down at the other end of the bench. 'How do you do it?' she said.

Frederick only turned away: his ears began burning again.

'What gets at you?' she said.

'Don't know.'

'Someone coming it over you? I know another boy

who cries like you, but he's older. He knots himself up and bellows.'

'What's his name?'

'George.'

'Does he go to school?'

'Oh, lord, no; he's a boy at the place where I used to work.' She raised one arm, leaned back, and watched four celluloid bangles, each of a different colour, slide down it to her elbow joint, where they stuck. 'He doesn't know why he does it,' she said, 'but he's got to. It's as though he saw something. You can't ask him. Some people take him that way: girls do. I never did. It's as if he knew about something he'd better not. I said once, well, what just *is* it, and he said if he *could* tell me he wouldn't do it. I said, well, what's the *reason*, and he said, well, what's the reason not to? I knew him well at one time.'

Frederick spat out two pips, looked round cautiously for the keeper, then dropped the apple-core down the back of the seat. 'Where'd George live?'

'I don't know now,' she said, 'I often wonder. I got sacked from that place where I used to work, and he went right off and I never saw him again. You snap out of that, if you can, before you are George's age. It does you no good. It's all the way you see things. Look, there's your mother back. Better move, or there'll be *more* trouble.' She held out her hand to Frederick, and when he put his in it shook hands so cheerfully, with such tough decision, that the four celluloid bangles danced on her wrist. 'You and George,' she said. 'Funny to meet two of you. Well, goodbye, Henry: cheer up.'

'I'm Frederick.'

'Well, cheer up, Freddie.'

As Frederick walked away, she smoothed down the sandwich papers inside her dispatch case and snapped the case shut again. Then she put a finger under her hair at each side, to tuck her spectacles firmly down on her ears. Her mouth, an unreddened line across her harshly-burnt face, still wore the same truculent, homely smile. She crossed her arms under the flat chest, across her stomach, and sat there holding her elbows idly, wagging one foot in its fawn sandal, looking fixedly at the lake through her spectacles, wondering about George. She had the afternoon, as she had no work. She saw George's face lifted abjectly from his arms on a table, blotchy over his clerk's collar. The eyes of George and Frederick seemed to her to be wounds, in the world's surface, through which its inner, terrible unassuageable, necessary sorrow constantly bled away and as constantly welled up.

Mrs. Dickinson came down the walk under the band of trees, carefully unanxious, looking lightly at objects to see if Frederick were near them: he had been a long time. Then she saw Frederick shaking hands with a sort of girl on a bench and starting to come her way. So she quickly turned her frank, friendly glance on the lake, down which, as though to greet her, a swan came swimming. She touched her fox fur lightly, sliding it up her shoulder. What a lovely mother to have. 'Well, Frederick,' she said, as he came into earshot, 'coming?' Wind sent a puff of red mayflowers through the air. She stood still and waited for Frederick to come up. She could not think what to do now: they had an hour to put in before they were due at Aunt Mary's. But this only made her manner calmer and more decisive.

Frederick gave a great skip, opened his mouth wide, shouted: 'Oo, I say, mother, I nearly caught a duck!'

'Frederick, dear, how silly you are: you couldn't.'

'Oo, yes, I could, I could. If I'd had salt for its tail!' Years later, Frederick could still remember, with ease, pleasure and with a sense of lonely shame being gone, that calm, white duck swimming off round the bank. But George's friend with the bangles, and George's trouble, fell through a cleft in his memory and were forgotten soon.

A WALK IN THE WOODS

THE mysterious thing was that the woods were full of people – though they showed a front of frondy depth and silence, inviolable and sifted through with sun. They looked like a whole element, like water, possible to behold but not to enter, in which only the native creature can exist. But this was a deception. Once inside them, it was only at a few moments that the solitary walker could feel himself alone, and lovers found it hard to snatch unregarded kisses. For those few moments when nobody was in sight, the glades of bronze bracken, the wet, green rides leading off still seemed to be the edge of another world. The brown distances, the deep hollows welled with magic, forlorn silence, as though they were untrodden. But what was likely to be the last fine Sunday of autumn had brought Londoners, or people from suburbs on this side of the city, in hundreds into these woods, which lay open, the People's property – criss-crossed by tarmac roads on which yellow leaves stuck. The people who came here were mostly well-to-do, for you needed a car to get here without effort. So saloon cars, run off the roads between the wide-apart birch-trees, were packed flank to flank, like shining square-rumped tin pigs, in the nearby glades. Inside a few of these cars people remained sitting with the wireless on – but mostly they had got out, yawned, stretched, and scattered in threes and fours.

Most of the Londoners lacked a sense of direction. Directly they were out of the sight of the road, an atavistic fear of the woods invaded them. Willing or unwilling they walked in circles, coming back again and again to make certain they had not lost their cars – in which had often been left a tea-basket, an overcoat of some value, or an old lady, an aunt or a grandmother. Not to be sure where one is induces panic – and yet the sensation of being lost was what they unconsciously looked for on this holiday – they had come to the woods. The sounds of bolder people whistling to dogs, of mackintoshes rustling against the bracken reassured them and made them strike in deeper.

Walking between the pillars of the trees, the men squared their shoulders – as though they inherited savage dignity. The matronly women, heavy in fur coats – which, just taken out after the summer, shed a smell of camphor – protestingly rolled as they walked on their smart heels. They looked about them, dissatisfied, acquisitive, despising the woods because they belonged to everyone. Had they not profoundly dreaded to trespass, they would have preferred the property of some duke. Now and then, recalling a pottery vase at home, they would strip off their gloves and reach for a fanlike spray of gold beech leaves. Or, unwillingly stooping, they tugged at a frond of bracken – but that is hard to pick. Their faces stayed unrelaxed: there is no poetry for the middle-class woman in her middle years. Nature's disturbing music is silent for her; her short phase of instinctive life is over. She is raising, forcing upward the children she has, and driving her man on. Her features become bleak with narrow inten-

tion: she is riveted into society. Still, to touch the edge
of Nature stands for an outing – you pack baskets and
throng to the edge of forest or sea. The still, damp,
glittering woods, the majestic death of the year were
reflected in the opaque eyes of these women – hardly
more human, very much less pathetic, than the glass eyes
of the foxes some of them wore. In family parties the
women and men parted; they did not speak to each other.
The women walked more slowly to act as a brake. Where
tracks narrowed between thickets or bracken the families
went in files. The children escaped and kept chasing
each other, cat-calling, round the trees. They were not
allowed to run down the wet, green rides.

Sometimes the thud of hooves was heard, and young
people on horseback crossed the end of a glade – in
coloured jerseys, with chins up, flaunting their bold
happiness. The walkers, with a sort of animal envy,
lowered their eyes and would not look after them.
From couples of lovers crashing through the bracken,
or standing suspended in love, fingers touching, in
patches of sun, eyes were averted in a commenting way.

The riders thudding across a glade were heard, not
seen, by a couple in a thicket. These two, in a secret
clearing at the foot of an oak, sat on a mackintosh eating
sandwiches. They were very hungry. They had come
to the edge of the woods in a Green Line bus, struck in
and wandered for a long time now, looking for the place
their fancy wanted. The woman, a city woman, refused
to believe the woods had no undiscovered heart, if one
could only come on it. Each time she had sighted the
black of another tarmac road she had let out a persecuted
sigh. The young man saw she was flagging, and he was
hungry. He had found what she wanted by fighting

through this thicket to the foot of the oak, then pulling her after him. In here they at least *saw* no one. They had spread the mackintosh, kissed, and opened the sandwiches.

'Listen,' she said. 'There go people riding.'

'Did you ever ride?'

'I did once.'

'On that farm?'

'Yes, that time,' she said, smiling quickly, touched that he should remember. She spoke often about her childhood, never about her girlhood – which was past, for she was ten years older than he. And her girlhood had been brief: she had married young. She watched him reach out for another sandwich, then gently and wilfully detained him by making her thumb and finger into a bracelet round his thin wrist. He pulled his wrist up to his lips and kissed the joint of her thumb. They enjoyed this play as seriously as lions. She shut her eyes, dropped her head back to let the sun through the branches fall on her forehead – then let his wrist go. He took the sandwich he wanted; she opened her eyes and saw him. 'You greedy boy.'

'Yes, I *am* greedy,' he said. '*You* know I'm greedy.'

She thrust both hands up her cheeks and said: 'That's no good – *here*.'

'No, we've struck unlucky. I thought woods in winter——'

'It's still autumn. It's the fine Sunday.' Her face went narrow, as though she heard the crack of a whip: she opened a gap in their thicket by bending a branch back. With cautious, angry eyes they both looked through. A party of five people were filing through the bracken, about ten yards away. 'There they go,' she said. 'There go the neighbours. That's my life. Oh, God! Henry——'

'They can't hurt us.'

'You know they can. Look, eat that last sandwich, do.'

'What about you?'

'I don't want it: I cut them for you. Turkey and ham, that should be.'

'*I'm* a spoilt boy,' said Henry, taking the sandwich without any more fuss. She crumpled up the paper, drove it with the point of his stick into the soft earth at the foot of the oak and earthed it up alive. Then she brushed crumbs from the mackintosh with a downcast face, making a bed in which they dare not lie. But Henry drew his long legs up, scrambled round like a dog and lay across the mackintosh with his head in Carlotta's lap. She stroked his stubborn dark hair back, leaned her bosom over his face and stroked his forehead with a terrible held-in tenderness. The whole weight of his body seemed to have gone into his head, which lay as heavy as a world on her thighs. His clerk's face was exposed to her touch and to the sky – generally so intent, over-expressive, nervous, the face was wiped into blank repose by her touch. He flung one hand across his chest and held a fold of her skirt. His spectacles, by reflecting the sky's light, hid his eyes from her, so she leaned over further and lifted them off gently. She looked into the blotted darkness of his pupils which, from being exposed like this, looked naked. Then he shut his eyes and put on the withdrawn smile of someone expecting sleep. 'You are so good,' he said.

'Sleep then . . . go on, sleep. . . .'

'Will you?'

'Maybe. Sleep. . . .'

But she watched, with the bend of her spine against the tree, while he lay with his eyes shut. She saw that his will to sleep was a gentle way of leaving her for a little. She felt a tide of peace coming in – but then the tide turned: his forehead twitched. A bird trilled its unhopeful autumn song. He opened his eyes and said: 'It's awful, having no place.'

'But we make a place of our own.'

'But I get so tired – all this doesn't seem natural.'

'Oh, Henry – what's the good?'

'Well, *you've* often said that.'

'Then *you've* said, what's the good?'

'It was all very well at first,' he said, 'just knowing you. Just coming round to your place. Seeing you before Joe got back, or even with Joe. I used to like you to have a place of your own – that was why I'd rather go with you than a girl.'

'That's what you want,' she said, 'just mothering. That's what Joe thinks; he doesn't think any harm. "Here comes your boy," he says. I think he's right, too: that's all you're really after.' She gently outlined his mouth with one of her fingertips.

But his mouth tightened. 'No, it's more than that now,' he said. '*You* know it's more than that.' He stared at the sky with his unfocused eyes – like a hare's eyes. 'I wanted what I've got; I wanted that all the time; I wanted that from the first – though it may once have been mixed up in the other thing. But ever *since* that, ever since we——'

'Do you wish we hadn't?'

'You don't know what you're saying. But I used to like your home; it was such a snug little place. I was happy there in a way: that's all gone now. I used to

42

like Joe, too, one time. And now – it's awful . . . *This* isn't what I imagined the first time I saw you. Hiding in woods like this – it isn't fit for you . . . really.'

'It's my only life. You're my only life. My only way out. Before you came, I was walled in alive. I didn't know where to turn. I was burning myself out . . . I don't mind where we go, so long as we get *away* from them . . . And we do have these days when Joe's gone to his mother's.'

'But we've got no place . . . When I was young I used to believe there was really some tremendous world, and that one would get to it. A sort of a Shakespeare world. And I heard it in music, too. And I lived there for three days after I first met you. I once used to believe——'

'But you're young still.'

'Well, perhaps I do still.'

'I always have. That's our place.'

'But we ought to have some real place – I mean, I want you.'

'Oh, shut up,' she said. 'I——'

'Look, come on,' he said, getting up. 'Better walk on. This does no good. Let's walk on into the woods.'

'They're so full.'

'But they look empty.'

'Kiss once——'

They kissed. It was he who pulled apart. He gathered up her mackintosh on his arm and began to fight a way out for her through the thickets. As she stepped between the branches he held back, her lips shook and she looked quite blind. Her look attracted the notice of Muffet and Isabella, two schoolgirls who, walking arm-in-arm through the woods, had already started to stare and nudge

43

each other on seeing the thicket of purple leaves shake. Any man and woman together made them giggle. They saw a haggard woman with dark red hair and a white face: something in her expression set them off giggling all the more. Henry disentangled the mackintosh from the last of the thicket; his consciousness of the girls staring and giggling made him look very young. His pride in Carlotta was wounded; his pity for her abased him. She was a married woman out with her neighbour's lodger. They both came from a newly developed suburb, and had met at the local debating society.

As he saw the girls' pink faces stuck open with laughter he saw why Carlotta hated her life. He saw why she towered like a statue out of place. She was like something wrecked and cast up on the wrong shore. When they met she had been one of these women going through life dutifully, and at the same time burning themselves up. Across the hall where they met, her forehead like no other woman's forehead, her impatient carriage, her deep eyes and held-in mouth, had been like a signal to him. He could not turn away. When they had talked, she excited, released, soothed him. Pride and a bitter feeling of misdirection had, up to that meeting, isolated them both. Passion broke down a wall in each of their lives. But her spirit was stronger than his, and so he was frightened of her . . . Carlotta stumbled stepping out of the thicket, and put a hand on his elbow for support. Henry twitched his elbow away and strode ahead of her, lashing round at the bracken with his stick.

'Henry——'

'Look out, they're looking. Those girls behind. *Don't* look round——'

'All right,' she said. 'We can't be too careful, can we.'
Henry did not know if she spoke in irony or sheer
pain.

Muffet was spending the Sunday with Isabella, whose
family lived not far from the Green Line bus stop. The
girls were friends at the High School. They both wore
dark-blue overcoats and walked bare-headed; their
lively faces showed no particular character. They were
allowed by their mothers to walk in the woods so long as
they did not get talking to men: they had been told
what happens to girls who do that – their minds were
bulging with cautionary horrors. They had neither of
them got boys yet: when they had got boys they would
stop walking together. At present their walks were gay
and enjoyable – on fine Sundays the woods were a great
show for them: too soon this would be over, winter silence
would fall.

This afternoon, in a fairly retired glade, they had
come on a lonely car in which a couple embraced. They
also inspected cars parked nearer the roadside, squinting
in at grandmothers and the picnic baskets, running
away in alarm from pairs of well-got-up women, upright
in backs of cars like idols under glass cases, discontentedly
waiting for their men to return. Or, intercepting a bar
of wireless music, Isabella and Muffet would take a few
dancing steps. They envied the thundering riders, the
young lovers, the imperious owners of well-bred dogs . . .
Isabella and Muffet, anything but reluctant, hopped
with impatience where brook and river meet. They
were fifteen. They stared at everyone. At the same
time they had a sense of propriety which was very easily
offended.

They peered at the broken thicket, then turned to stare after the couple.

'My goodness,' said Isabella, '*she* looked silly!'

'Breaking trees, too,' said Muffet. 'That's against the law.'

'Besides being old enough to be his mother. She *was* old. Did you see her?'

'Perhaps she was his mother.'

'Mother my eye! But he gave her the push all right – did you see that? Did you see?'

'Going on at him like that.'

'Well, I call it a shame. It's a shame on him. He's a nice boy.'

'No, I call him sappy. I mean, at her age. Fancy him letting her.'

'Well, I tell you, I call it a shame.'

'Well, I tell you, it makes me laugh . . . Look, let's go down there: I see people down there.' Isabella dug a bag of sweets out of her pocket and they sauntered on, both sucking, talking with cheeks blocked. 'Supposing you got offered a fur coat, what kind would you go for, nutria or kolinsky? . . . If a boy that always went racing but that you were sweet on asked you to marry him, would you? . . . Supposing you were going with a boy, then found out he was a trunk murderer . . .'

'Oh, there's such a sweet dog, such a sweet fellow. Come, then!'

'My goodness,' said Isabella, 'it isn't half getting dark.'

'Well, what *do* you expect?'

'No, but the sun's gone in. And that's not mist, now; that's fog, that is.'

'They're starting two of those cars up.'

'Mother'll be starting to worry. Better be getting home.'

Yes, mist that had been the natural breath of the woods was thickening to fog, as though the not-distant city had sent out an infection. At dusk coming so suddenly and so early, the people felt a touch of animal fear – quickening their steps, they closed on each other in a disordered way, as though their instinct were to bolt underground. Wind or thunder, though more terrible in woods, do not hold this same threat of dissolution. The people packed back into their cars; the cars lurched on to the roads and started back to London in a solid stream. Down the rides, beginning to be deserted, the trees with their leaves still clinging looked despoiled and tattered. All day the woods had worn an heroic dying smile; now they were left alone to face death.

But this was still somebody's moment. There was still some daylight. The small lake, or big pool, clearly reflected in its black mirror the birches and reeds. A tall girl, with a not quite young porcelain face, folding her black fur collar round her throat with both hands, stood posing against a birch, having her photograph taken across the water by two young men at the other side of the lake. Bob, busy over the camera on a portable tripod, was an 'art' photographer: he could photograph Nature in the most difficult light. Therefore he could go far in search of her strange moods. He felt, thought, loved, even, in terms of the Lens. He sold his work to papers, where it appeared with lines of poetry underneath. This girl over the water in the fog-smudged woods was to be called *Autumn Evening*. Cecil, an old friend, behind Bob's shoulder, looked across at the girl.

Without breaking her pose, a born model's, she coughed, and shook under her fur coat. Cecil said cautiously: 'She's getting a bit cold, Bob.'

'*Tsssss!*' said Bob sharply. He had become his camera. His whole temperament crouched over his subject, like a lion over a bit of meat.

'Won't be long,' Cecil called across the lake.

'I'm all right,' said the girl, coughing again.

'Tell her not to grab her collar up,' Bob muttered. 'She's not supposed to look cold. She's got her coat all dragged up; it spoils the figure.'

'He says, not to grab your collar,' Cecil shouted.

'Right-o.' She let her collar fall open. Turning her head inside the fur coralla, she looked more obliquely across the lake. 'Is that better?'

'O.K. . . . *Ready!*' The slow exposure began.

People taking photographs in this half-light, this dream-light, made Carlotta and Henry stop to wonder. They stood back among the birches to be out of the way. Then the artistic tensity broke up; signals were exchanged across the water; the girl came round the lake to join the two young men. 'What's that floating?' she said. But they were busy packing up the camera. 'Should that be all right?' she said, but no one answered. Bob handed Cecil the tripod, shouldered his camera, and they walked away from the lake with Bob's hand on his girl's shoulder.

'Do you think that photo will ever come out?' said Carlotta.

'I suppose he knows what he's doing . . . I'd like to try with a camera. . . .'

'I'd sooner paint,' said Carlotta. They walked round

the edge of the lake, looking across to where the girl had stood. 'She was pretty,' Carlotta said. She thought: 'She'll get her death. But I'd like to stand like that. I wish Henry *had* a camera. I wish I could give him one . . .' Against the photographer's shoulder-blade eternalized minutes were being carried away. Carlotta and Henry were both tired: what they saw seemed to belong in the past already. The light seemed to fade because of their own nerves. And still water in woods, in any part of the world, continues an everlasting terrible fairy tale, in which you are always lost, in which giants oppress. Now the people had gone, the lovers saw that this place was what they had been looking for all today. But they were so tired, each stood in an isolated dream.

'What *is* that floating?' she said.

Henry screwed up his eyes. 'A thermos.' He picked up a broken branch and, with an infinity of trouble, started to claw in, with the tip of the branch, the floating flask towards himself. Its cap was gone.

'But we don't want it, Henry.'

She might never have spoken – Henry's face was intent; he recklessly stood with one toe in the water. The ribbed aluminium cylinder, twirling under the touches of the branch, rode reluctantly in. Henry reached it eagerly out of the water, shook it. Its shattered inner glass coating rattled about inside – this, the light hollowness, the feel of the ribs in his grasp made Henry smile with almost crazy pleasure. 'Treasure!' he said, with a checked, excited laugh.

Carlotta smiled, but she felt her throat tighten. She saw Henry's life curve off from hers, like one railway line from another, curve off to an utterly different and far-off destination. When she trusted herself to speak, she said as gently as possible: 'We'll have to be starting back soon. You know it's some way. The bus——'

'No, we won't miss that,' said Henry, rattling the flask and smiling.

A LOVE STORY
1939

MIST lay over the estuary, over the terrace, over
the hollows of the gummy, sub-tropical garden
of the hotel. Now and then a soft, sucking sigh
came from the water, as though someone were turning
over in his sleep. At the head of the steps down to the
boathouse, a patch of hydrangeas still flowered and rotted,
though it was December. It was now six o'clock, dark —
chinks of light from the hotel lay yellow and blurred
on the density. The mist's muffling silence could be
everywhere felt. Light from the double glass doors fell
down the damp steps. At the head of the steps the cast-
iron standard lamps were unlit.

Inside the double glass doors, the lounge with its
high curtained bow windows was empty. Brilliantly
hotly lit by electric light, it looked like a stage on which
there has been a hitch. Light blared on the *vieux rose*
curtains and on the ocean of carpet with its jazz design.
The armchairs and settees with their taut stuffing had
an air of brutal, resilient strength. Brass ashtrays without a segment of ash stood on small tables dotted over
the lounge. A glass screen kept the lounge from any
draughts from the door; a glass screen protected the
lounge from the stairs. But there was nothing to dread:
the heating was on, only a smell of tinder-dry turkey

carpet, ivory paint, polish and radiators came downstairs from the empty floors above. In the immense tiled fireplace a fire burned with a visible, silent roar.

From a cabinet came a voice announcing the six o'clock war news. In the middle of this, three berries fell from a vase of holly and pattered noisily into a brass tray. The temperate voice of the announcer paused for a moment, half-way through a disaster, as though disturbed by the noise. A spurt of gas from a coal sent a whicker up through the fire. The unheard news came to an end.

Two women came up the steps and pushed in at the glass doors. Their hair was sticky from the damp of the mist. The girl steered her mother round the screen to the fire, then went across and turned off the wireless. The mother unbuttoned her leather coat and threw it back from her handsome, full chest. Keyed up by the sudden electric light, her manner was swaggering and excitable. She looked with contempt at the wireless cabinet and said: 'I don't care what I hear – now!'

'Do shut up, mother. Do sit down.'

'Do stop being so nervous of me, Teresa. Whatever do you think I'm going to do?'

Teresa took off her trenchcoat and slung it over a chair, then crossed the lounge with her loose, cross walk, in her slacks. 'I know what you want,' she said flatly, ringing the bell. She sat down in an armchair by the fire and stuck her young slender jaw out and crossed her legs. Her mother stayed standing up, with her shoulders braced back; she kept pushing her hair back from her forehead with her long, plump, fine-wristed ringed hand. 'I daresay you're right to be so nervous,' she said. 'I don't know myself what I'll do, from minute to minute.

52

Why did I have to come here – can you tell me that? Why was this the only thing I could do? Do you know when I was last here – who I was with?'

'I suppose I know,' said Teresa, defensively. 'You know you don't want me to understand you, mother, so I'm not trying to.'

'It's a terrible thing to say,' said Mrs. Massey, 'but it would be better if this had happened to you. I'd rather see you suffer than have no feelings. You're not like a woman, Teresa. And he was your age, not my age.'

'Is that so?' Teresa said, in a voice too lifeless for irony.

Mrs. Massey looked angrily round the lounge and said: 'They've changed the chairs round, since.' She pointed to an empty space on the carpet and said: '*That* was where he sat . . . There isn't even his chair.'

Teresa looked pointedly off down the corridor. 'Michael's coming,' she said. A boy in a white cotton coat, with a dark, vivid, Kerry face, beamed at them through the glass screen, then came round the screen for orders. 'Good evening, Michael,' said Teresa.

'Good evening, miss. Good evening to you, ma'am.'

'It's not a good evening for me, I'm afraid, Michael.'

Michael lowered his eyes. 'I'm sorry to hear that,' he said, in a trembling and feeling voice. 'It's a long time since we saw you.'

'Does it seem so——?' Mrs. Massey began wildly. But Teresa put up her hand and in a curt, raised voice ordered her mother's drink . . . 'But I wanted a double,' objected Mrs. Massey, when Michael had gone.

'You know you had that at home,' said Teresa, 'and more than once.' More coldly, she added: 'And how fed up Teddy used to get.'

Frank and Linda, their fingers loosely linked, came downstairs on their way to their private sitting-room. They glanced vacantly through the screen and turned left down the corridor. 'We missed the news again,' she said, as he shut the door. 'We always seem to run late.' 'We can't help that, darling,' he said. Their fire had been made up while they were upstairs. She gave it an unnecessary kick with her heel, and said: 'Did you see those two making a scene in the lounge?'

'I sort of did see the girl,' Frank said. 'Which was the other?'

'I thought they looked like locals in for a drink. Or I daresay they came round here to make a scene. I do think the Irish are exhibitionists.'

'Well, we can't help that, darling, can we?' said Frank, ringing the bell. He sat down in a chair and said: 'Oh, my God . . .' Linda dropping into the chair opposite. 'Well, really . . .' Frank said. 'However, I feel fine. I don't care what time it is.'

Up in a sitting-room on the first floor, the Perry-Duntons' two dogs slept in front of the fire, bellies taut to the heat. Legs rigid, they lay in running attitudes, like stuffed dogs knocked over on to their sides. On the sofa pulled up opposite the fire was Clifford – feet braced against one end, backbone against the other, knees up, typewriter in the pit of his stomach, chin tucked down into his chest. With elbows in to his ribs in a trussed position, he now and then made a cramped dash at the keys. When the keys stopped, he stayed frowning at them. Sheet after sheet, completed without conviction, fluttered on to the hearthrug between the dogs.

Polly Perry-Dunton's armchair was pushed up so that

one arm made telepathic contact with Clifford's sofa. Curled up childishly in the cushions, she held a Penguin volume a little above her face. She kept the stiff Penguin open by means of an anxious pressure from her thumb. She read like someone told to pose with a book, and seemed unable to read without holding her breath.

Crackles came now and then from the *Daily Sketch* that Clifford had folded under his feet. Light blazed on their two heads from a marble bowl near the ceiling. The top of the mantelpiece was stacked with Penguins; the other armchair was stacked with American magazines. Polly's portable wireless in its shagreen cover stood silent on the floor by her chair. An art photograph of Clifford and Polly, profiles just overlapping like heads on a coin, was propped on the whatnot and kept from slipping by Polly's toy panda from Fortnum's.

Clifford reached out his right hand, apparently vaguely: Polly uncoiled like a spring from the armchair, knelt on the hearthrug and lit him a cigarette. Cigarette pressed tightly between his lips, Clifford turned back to frown at the keys again. She sat back on her heels to adore his frown, his curls, his fresh skin – then she locked her arms tightly around his neck. The impulsive, light little-girlishness of the movement let him still say nothing, not even turn his head.

She said into his cheek: 'May Polly say one thing?'

'Mm-mm.'

'I've left my pussy gloves in the car.'

'Mm-mm . . . You don't want them, do you?'

'No, not indoors. I wouldn't want gloves indoors. But let's remember tomorrow . . . Look, you crumpled one sheet right up. Did you mean to?'

'I meant to.'

Polly reverently uncrumpled the sheet. 'Pity,' she said. 'It's beautifully typed. Do you mean you're *not* going to say all that?'

'No. I'm trying to think of something else.'

'I should think most people could never think of so much that they were even not going to say.'

Clifford waited a minute, then he unfastened Polly's arms from his neck with as little emotion as a woman undoing a boa. He then typed five or six lines in a sort of rush. She returned with a glutted sigh to her chair, thumbed her book, held her breath and thought of her pussy gloves.

Clifford's voice to Polly was always the same: resignation or irony kept it on one note. The two of them had been over here on honeymoon when the war began; here they still were, because of the war. Some days he went out with his gun along the foot of the mountain, some days they ran the motor-boat in and out of white inlets or to an island, some days they went out in Polly's big car. When they had run the car back into the lock-up they would walk back, her hand creeping inside his, down the tarmac curve to the hotel between walls of evergreen. At this hour, the tarmac gleamed wet-white in the lasting, luminous Irish dusk. From this hour, claustrophobia resumed its sway. Polly hardly reached up to Clifford's shoulders; she walked beside him with her little skip-and-jump. She felt that his being so tall, she so little, cancelled out their adverse difference in age. She was thirty-two, he twenty-four. Her trim little sexless figure, her kilted skirts, socks and little-girl snooded hair that flopped forward so softly could make her look fourteen. Without the ring of technicians who got her up she could have easily looked faded and sluttish,

like a little girl in Woolworth's wilting behind the goods.
But she had a childish hard will, and by day she never
looked old.

She grew up when she was asleep. Then, a map of
unwilling adult awareness – lines, tensions and hollows –
appeared in her exposed face. Harsh sleep froze her
liquidity; her features assembled themselves and became
austere. An expression of watching wrote itself on the
lids of her shut eyes. The dread she denied all day came
out while she slept and stood in the door. The flittering
of a palm tree, the bump of a moored boat as the tide
rose, the collapse of a last coal in their grate went straight
to the nerves upright under her sleep. She slept
tenaciously, late into the daylight – but Clifford never
looked at her long.

Her rape of Clifford – with his animal muteness,
nonchalance, mystery and the charm of the obstination
of his wish to write – had been the climax of Polly's
first real wish. Her will had detected the flaw in his will
that made the bid possible. Her father had bought him
for her. Till they met, her wealth and her years of
styleless, backgroundless dullness had atrophied Polly.
The impulse with which she first put her arms round
Clifford's neck and told him never to leave her had been,
however, unforced and pure. Rain – a little rain, not
much – fell on her small parched nature at Clifford's
tentative kiss. There had seemed no threat to Polly in
Clifford's nature till the war came, with its masculine
threat. Their sequestration now, here, remained out-
wardly simple: Clifford handled no money, Polly drew all
the cheques.

They stayed on here where they were hidden and
easy – any move might end in some fatal way. The

Perry-Duntons knew almost nothing of the hotel. They had meals served in their suite, and only went down or upstairs or through the lounge on their way outdoors or in. During such appearances, Polly's service-flat temperament sheathed her in passive, moronic unseeing-ness. Her blindness made everything negative – Clifford saw nothing, either. He walked out or in through the public rooms beside her, tense, persecuted by the idea of notice, with his baited, defensive frown. The hotel had come to return the Perry-Duntons' indifference. The out-of-season skeleton staff of servants served them without interest, acting the automata Polly took them to be. Servants love love and money, but the Perry-Duntons bored the servants, by now. By now even Mrs. Coughlan, the manageress, thought and spoke of them with apathy. The Perry-Duntons deadened the air round them with their static, depleting intimacy.

Now, Clifford twitched one more sheet off the machine. Leaning sideways over from the sofa, he, with absorption, began to tickle a dog's belly with an edge of the sheet. The dog bent itself further backward, into a bow. Watchful, Polly judged that this meant a break. She got up and began to tug like a bird at the *Daily Sketch* under Clifford's feet. 'What's that there for?' she said. 'I don't think I've looked at it yet.'

'Sorry,' said Clifford, raising his feet.

'But what's it *there* for, Clifford?'

'I was taught not to put my boots up on things – not straight up on things, that is.'

'How funny, because you generally do. I wonder what made you just think of that?'

Clifford could not tell her. He swung his feet off the sofa on to the hearthrug between the dogs. Sitting forward on the edge of the sofa, elbows on his wide-apart knees, he dug his heels slowly, without passion, into the rug. He looked slowly down from his hands with their hanging bunches of fingers to the oriental pattern under them. Polly picked up a sheet of typewriting and began to read. 'Goodness,' she said, after an interval, 'I hope you're not going to *throw* this one away! . . . What's the matter?'

'I'm going out for your gloves.'

'Oh, but I don't want them.'

'I'd like to go out for them, rather. I'd like a stretch.'

'*Alone*, Clifford?'

'There's a mist.'

'You might get lost. You might walk into the water. Do you really *want* to go out?'

At this, the dogs got up and looked eager. He pushed at them with his feet. 'No, stay with Polly,' he said. 'I won't be long.'

'You do promise?' She folded herself way from him in an abandon of puzzled sadness. Clifford kicked the dogs back again and went quietly round the door.

Frank stepped across the corridor to the office to get a stamp for Linda. The plate-glass and mahogany front of the office was framed in tariffs of summer trips, sets of view postcards printed in dark blue and a bill of the working-hours of the Protestant church. The glass hatch was down: Frank put his face against it and looked flirtatiously into the back recess. On an inside ledge, the register was just out of view. Mrs. Coughlan put up the glass hatch, like a lady playing at keeping shop. She received the full blast of Frank's full-blooded charm. 'Stamp?' she said. 'Oh dear, now Miss Heally knows, where they are. To tell you the truth, I'm afraid I don't, and Miss Heally's just upstairs having a little rest. We're very quiet just now. Don't you find it terribly quiet – Major Mull?'

'Mr. Mull,' said Frank. 'Oh, we love it,' he said.

'Still, it's not like the season, is it? Will you be back with us then?'

'Will I not!' said Frank, using his eyes.

'Is the stamp for yourself?'

'Well, it's not: it's for my cousin.'

'Ah yes,' said Mrs. Coughlan, not batting an eyelid. 'The post went, you know; it went about five minutes. But I tell you what – Were you never in the last war?' – 'I was,' said Frank. 'But I'm not in this one, thank God.' – 'Now Miss Heally thought you had some military rank – I tell you what I could do, I could let you have a stamp I have, if I could trouble you to step this way.'

She pressed with her corsets against the door of the counter, and Frank let her out. She preceded him down the warm, half-lit, spongey-carpeted corridor to the door of her sitting-room: from this, she recoiled on to Frank's toe, at the same time blowing a whisper in at his right ear. 'I won't ask you in here,' she said, 'if you don't mind. I've a lady in here who is a little upset.' As she spoke, the door of the sitting-room opened, and the, to Frank's eye, snappy form of Teresa appeared, outlined in electric light. Teresa glowered at Frank, then said: 'We'll be going now, Mrs. Coughlan. I think my mother would really rather be home.'

'I would not rather!' exclaimed unseen Mrs. Massey. 'For God's sake, Teresa, let me alone.'

'No, don't let me barge in,' said Frank, standing firmly just where he was. Mrs. Coughlan flashed at him

the recognition that *he* would be always the gentleman.
'Well, if you'll excuse me,' she said, 'for just a jiffy,
I'll bring the stamp along to your sitting-room.'

Frank went back to Linda. He left their door an inch
open and, while they were waiting, rang for a glass of
port. 'What's that for?' said Linda. 'I wanted a stamp.'

'That's for Mrs. Coughlan. You'll get your stamp to
play with. But of course you know that the post's gone?'
'Then hell, what is the good of a stamp?' 'You said you
wanted a stamp, so I'm getting a stamp for you. I love
getting you anything that you want.' 'Then what's the
point of me having written this letter?' 'None, darling;
I told you that. Writing letters is just fidgets. Never
mind, it will come in some time when you want a letter
to post.'

Disengaging herself from Frank's kiss, Linda propped
the letter up on the mantelpiece, on a carton of cigarettes.
While he kissed her again, she looked at it out of one
eye. This made Frank look too. 'Oh, *that's* who it's to,'
he said. He made faces at it, while Linda, still held
pressed to his chest, giggled contentedly. 'I sort of had
to,' she said, 'or he wouldn't know where I am.'

Mrs. Coughlan came in with the stamp. The port
was brought in by Michael and put on the mantelpiece.
She started at it, but after a certain amount of fuss was
induced to lift her glass daintily. 'Well, here's to you,'
she said. 'And to you too,' she said to Linda. 'But isn't
this really dreadful, at this hour.'

'Good for the heart,' said Frank. 'Not that your heart
needs it, I'm sure. But your caller sounded to me a bit
off.'

'Oh, Mrs. Massey's had bad news. She came round
here with her daughter, then didn't feel well.'

'Was she in the lounge?' said Linda.

'She was first, but it didn't seem fit for her, so Miss Teresa made her come into me. You don't know who might come into a public room. So I said, to come in to me for a little rest, while I kept an eye on the office while Miss Heally was up. We are all devoted to Mrs. Massey,' said Mrs. Coughlan, meeting the eye of Linda just a shade stonily. 'I was saying to Miss Heally only this morning, wasn't it too long since we'd seen Teresa or her. They're in and out, as a rule, with the friends Mrs. Massey has staying. They're quite near to here, through the woods, though it's longer if you take the two avenues. They've a sweet place, there, but it's lonely; they've nothing there but the sea.'

'Through the woods?' said Linda. 'Then, do you mean that pink house? – That's that house *we* want,' she said to Frank. Mrs. Coughlan glanced primly midway between the two of them. 'Yes, it's a sweet place, Palmlawn,' said Mrs. Coughlan. 'We often say, she seems quite wedded to it.'

Frank said: 'Is Teresa the tiger cat?'

Far too much won by Frank's eye and manner, Mrs. Coughlan had to pause to prop up her loyalties. 'Well, her manner's just a weeshy bit short,' she said. 'And this evening, of course, *she's* upset, too.'

'She sounded more fed up.'

Mrs. Coughlan, replacing her glass on the mantel-piece, dabbed her mouth with an *eau de nil* handkerchief charged with *Muguet de Coty*. Reassembling herself as manageress, she threw an inventorial glance round their sitting-room. 'I hope,' she said, 'you have every-thing? Everything comfy? Ring if it isn't, won't you?'

'Yes, thanks,' said Linda, 'we're very cosy in here.'

Mrs. Coughlan, whose business it was to know how to take everything, knew perfectly well how to take this. 'Well, I must be running along. Thank you very much, Major Mull – Mr. Mull – I hope you'll join *me* for a minute or two this evening, unless, of course, you're engaged . . . Isn't this war shocking?'

'Shocking,' said Frank. 'I sell cars.'

'Very,' said Linda. 'Why?'

'I can't help thinking,' said Mrs. Coughlan, 'of poor Mrs. Massey's friend. A flying man. He was often in here, you know.'

Fumbling with the slimy lock in the mist, Clifford unlocked the lock-up. He reached into the Alvis, switched the dashboard lights on and got in and sat in the car to look for Polly's gloves. Mist came curdling into the lock-up after him. He put the wrist-length, fluffy gloves in one pocket. Then he checked up on the petrol: there were six gallons still. Then he plunged his hand slowly into another of his pockets, touched the pennies, thumbed the two half-crowns. In the dark his body recorded, not for the first time, yet another shock of the recurrent idea. The shock, as always, dulled out. He switched the lights off, folded his arms, slid forward and sat in the dark deflated – completely deflated, a dying pig that has died.

Frank and Linda, intently, silently cosy in front of their sitting-room fire in the dark, heard people break into the passage from Mrs. Coughlan's room. At this Frank, with pussy-cat stealth and quickness, raised his face from the top of Linda's head. His clean ears, close to his head, might have been said to prick up. 'Damn,' said

Linda, missing Frank, 'something is always happening.'
The concourse passed their door. 'That's Mrs. Massey,
that was.' Frank at once pressed his hands on Linda's
shoulders. But he said: 'Should I just have a look-see?'
He got up, padded across the room, opened the door an
inch and put one eye to the inch.

Mrs. Coughlan had not gone far. She immediately
came back and put her mouth into the inch of door.
'Mr. Mull, could I trouble you just a minute?' she said.
Frank edged round the door and Linda was left alone.

Mrs. Massey was not equal to the walk back. This –
only felt by herself as an additional rush of sorrow – was
clear to Teresa, and also to Mrs. Coughlan, as a predicament. There had been talk, before they left Mrs.
Coughlan's parlour, of telephoning to the village for a
car. Mrs. Massey would not brook the idea. 'I won't
give trouble,' she said. 'There's trouble enough already.'
Magnificent with protest, she now stood trembling and
talking loudly and sweeping her hair back at the foot of
the stairs. 'I should never have come,' she said. 'But
how could I stay where I was? We'll go home now;
we'll just go quietly home – Are you gummed there,
Teresa? Come home: we've been here quite long
enough.' She gave Frank a haunted look as Mrs.
Coughlan brought him up. 'This is Mr. Mull, Mrs.
Massey,' said Mrs. Coughlan. 'Mr. Mull says he'll just
get his car out and run you home.'

Mrs. Massey said: 'I don't know what you all think.'

Teresa, taking no notice, put on her trenchcoat and
tightly buckled the belt. 'That is good of you,' she said
to Frank slightingly. 'Aren't you busy?' 'Not in the
world,' said Frank. 'Hold on while I get the car round.'

'You needn't do that, thank you: Mother and I can walk as far as the car.'

Teresa and Frank, with Mrs. Massey between them, started off down the aisle of carpet to the glass doors. 'Aren't the steps dreadfully dark for her!' helped Miss Heally, who was there with the rest – she shot ahead to switch on the outdoor lamps. The three passed down the steps in the blur of a blaze of lights, as though leaving a ball. 'Good night now. Safe home, Mrs. Massey dear!' called Miss Heally and Mrs. Coughlan from the top of the steps. Linda, hearing the noise, hearing Frank's step on the gravel, threw a window up and leaned into the mist. She called: 'Frank?' He replied if at all, with a gesture that she could not see: he was busy steering the party. 'Left turn,' he said, patting at Mrs. Massey's elbow. The mother and daughter wheeled docilely.

'Do you know where we are, at all?'

'Oh, I'm used to all this.'

'Do you come from London, then?' Teresa said.

'I've come back from London.'

'On leave?' said Teresa quickly.

'No, thank God. I sell cars.'

'You won't sell many just now.' Teresa's trenchcoat brushed on the evergreens. Majestic and dazed between her escort, Mrs. Massey stumbled along in a shackled way. In the yard, the open doors of the lock-up beside Frank's stuck out clammy into the mist: they almost walked into them. 'That lunatic's taken that Alvis out,' said Frank. Teresa, in her not encouraging way, said: 'Well, you'll be another lunatic, in a minute.' Mrs. Massey, ignoring the dialogue, detached herself quietly from Teresa. While Frank and his torch and key were busy over a padlock, Mrs. Massey passed quietly into the open lock-up next door. She bumped her knee on the Alvis and started to climb round it. 'It's all right, Teresa, the car's in here,' she called back, with quite an approach to her usual gaiety.

Clifford's reflex to the bump on the car was to blaze all his lights on. Inside, his lock-up became one curdled glare; his tail light spread a ruby stain on the mist. He turned his head sharply and stayed with his coinlike profile immobilized against the glaring end wall. Mrs. Massey came scrambling into view. Clifford put down one window. 'I beg your pardon?' he said.

'Better back out a little,' said Mrs. Massey. 'I can't get in this side while you're in here.' Clifford started his engine and backed out. But then he pulled up, got up and got half out of the car. 'I'm afraid this is not your car,' he said.

'How could it be my car,' said Mrs. Massey, 'when my car's at home? This is so kind of you – I don't know what you must think. Let me in now, though.' Clifford shrank back; she got in and settled herself by him contentedly. 'There's my daughter to come,' she said, 'and a man from the hotel. Just wait, now, and they'll show you the way.'

Frank had only just got his lock-up open when Teresa was at his elbow again. 'We'll hang on a minute,' he said, 'and let this other chap out. I'll start up. Be getting your mother in at the back.'

'My mother's got into the other car.'

'Which car?'

'I don't know. Don't dawdle there – are you mad? Mother might be off anywhere!'

Frank went out to blink. The Alvis, almost silently turning, swept a choked glare through the mist. 'Oh, *that* chap,' Frank said. 'That chap won't eat anyone. Cut along, Teresa – look, he's waiting for you.'

'I don't know him.'

'Mother knows him by now.'

'You're well out of us,' said Teresa, standing still bitterly.

'If that's what you think,' Frank said, 'I'll come along too.'

Linda was told of Frank's kindness in volunteering to drive the Masseys home. Mrs. Coughlan was very much pleased and could not praise him enough. He should be back at the hotel in twenty minutes – but Linda knew he would not be. Frank's superabundance of good feeling made Linda pretty cross – his gusto, his sociability, his human fun, and his conquering bossiness. He liked life, and wherever he was things happened. This evening, first Mrs. Coughlan, now Mrs. Massey . . . Except in bed, one was seldom alone with Frank. Having interfered once more, and got one more kind act in, he would come back like a cat full of rabbit again. Linda felt quite suspended. She wished there were pin tables in this high-class hotel. She rang for a drink and two packs of cards and sat down and laid out a complex patience on the octagonal table below the sitting-room light. She thanked God she was not as young as she had been and no longer fell into desperations or piques. It was not that Frank did not concentrate, but he did not concentrate consecutively. She looked up once from her patience at her stamped letter, and half thought of tearing it up and writing a warmer one.

Mrs. Coughlan and Miss Heally returned to their sitting-room: opening the piano they began to play a duet.

Polly Perry-Dunton, as well as Linda, heard the piano. Every three minutes Polly looked at her watch. After ten minutes, Polly left her sitting-room and went and lay on her bed in a sort of rigour. She pulled Clifford's pyjamas out from under the pillow and buried her face in them.

The Alvis, dip lights squinting along the row of sticky trees on the left, nosed its way through the mist down the avenue. Mrs. Massey, in absolute quiescence, leaned back by Clifford's shoulder: he drove in silence. Frank, in the back of the car beside Teresa, had noncommittally drawn her arm through his. Teresa did not take her eyes from the back of her mother's head. When the open white gates loomed up, Teresa leaned forward and told Clifford which way to turn. About a mile down the main road Teresa again spoke up. Clifford turned through more gates, and the four of them passed with well-sprung smoothness over the bumps of a peaty wet avenue. An uneasy smell of the sea came up the mist. Rhododendrons lolled and brushed the sides of the car. The left wheels mounted an edge of lawn. Clifford took a sweep and undipped his lights on veranda-posts and the pallid walls of a house.

'Teresa,' said Mrs. Massey, 'tell them to come in.'

Teresa lit the two oil lamps under their dark pink shades. Mrs. Massey, one hand on her drawing-room mantel-piece, swayed with the noble naturalness of a tree. Her form, above a smoulder of peat fire, was reflected in a mirror between the two dark windows – a mirror that ran from ceiling to floor. The room with its posses-sions, its air of bravura and slipshod moodiness, its low, smoked ceiling, armchairs with sunk seats, cabinets of dull glass began to be seen in the dark light. Clifford's scraggy Nordic figure, and Frank's thick-set springy figure, firmly poised on its heels, were also seen in the mirror, making a crowd.

'Sit down,' said Mrs. Massey, 'I feel more like standing. I'm afraid I'm restless – I had bad news, you know.'

'That is frightfully tough,' said Frank.

'I feel bad,' said Mrs. Massey, 'at not knowing your names. Yes, it's tough to be dead isn't it? He was about your age,' she said to Clifford. ' – Teresa dear, are you gummed there? Go and look for the drinks.'

Through the shadows in which they were all still standing up, Clifford threw a quick, begging look at Frank. Frank had to defer to Clifford's panic, and to Clifford's being unable to speak. 'Look, we must be pushing along,' Frank reluctantly, firmly said. Clifford bowed his heroic head sharply and took two steps to the door: the nightmare of being wanted was beginning, in this room, to close in round him again.

Mrs. Massey only removed her eyes from Clifford to attend to a cigarette she was lighting over a lamp. Obliterated in shadows round the unglowing fire, Teresa, crouching, puffed at peat with a bellows. 'Teresa,' said her mother, 'do *you* see who he's so like——?'

' – There's no drink left, as you know,' said Teresa quickly. 'I could make some tea, but they're just off.'

Clifford said: 'I'm afraid we *are* just off!'

In reply, Mrs. Massey lifted the lamp from its low table to hold it, unsteadily, on a level with Clifford's face. She took a step or two forward, with the lamp. 'It's extraordinary,' she said, 'though you don't know it, that you should be in this house *tonight*. You mustn't mind what I say or do: I'm upset – you're English, too, aren't you? He looks like a hero, doesn't he?' she said appealingly to Frank.

'Now we've all had a look at each other,' said Frank firmly, 'let me take this out of your way.' Taking the wobbling lamp from Mrs. Massey, he put it safely back on its table again.

'I wish I were proud of my country,' said Mrs. Massey. 'But I'm ashamed of this country to tell you the truth.'

'Oh, come,' said Frank. 'We have much to be thankful for.'

Teresa crashed the bellows into the grate and went out of the room through the open door. Outside, she pulled up a chair and stood on it to light the lamp in the hall. Frank strolled after her and leaned in the door to watch. He said: 'Are you very fed up?' The hanging lamp spun round, and Teresa's eyes, fixed on the burner, glittered. 'Is it bad?' Frank said. 'You don't tell me anything. Did *you* love the poor chap?'

'Did I get a chance?'

The chair she stood on wobbled on the uneven flag-stones: Frank came and stood close up to steady the chair. 'Come down off that,' he said, 'like a good girl.' Teresa stepped down off the chair into Frank's arms – but she stood inside them like steel. He let her go, and watched her pick up her trenchcoat and walk off down a stone passage to hang it up. There she stayed, as though she were falling and could fall no further, with her breast and face thrust into the hanging coats. Her shoulder-blades showed through her sweater, and Frank, coming up gently, put his two hands on them. 'She'd rather him dead,' said Teresa into the coats, 'she'd rather him dead than gone from her.' She kept moving her shoulders under Frank's hands.

'Could you cry? Could you have a cry if I took you off now in that car?'

Teresa, into the coats, said something he could not hear. 'And leave those two?' she said in a louder voice.

Frank had to agree: he looked back at the drawing-room door.

Mrs. Massey and Clifford, waiting for Frank, now sat in two armchairs opposite the fire. 'I don't understand,' she said. 'How did we come in your car?'

'You got in . . .' he said tentatively.

'And where had you been going?'

'Nowhere; I was looking for my wife's gloves.' He pulled the pussy gloves out of his pocket and showed them, to show he spoke the truth. Looking intently at the pussy gloves, Mrs. Massey's eyes for the first time filled with tears. The access of some new feeling, a feeling with no context, resculptured her face. In the musty dark of her drawing-room, the dark round the dull fire, her new face looked alabaster and pure. The outline of her mist-clotted fair hair shook, as though shaken by the unconscious silent force of her tears.

'Aren't they small!' she said. 'Is your wife quite a little thing? Are you two very happy, then?'

'Very.'

'Take her gloves back safe . . . How English you are.'

Frank came in and said they must be pushing along. Teresa did not come in; she was opening the hall door. Out there on the sweep above the lawn and the sea, Clifford's lights were still blazing into the mist. Teresa went out and examined, as much by touch as anything, the wonderful car. An idea of going away for ever lifted and moved her heart, like a tide coming in. A whiteness up in the mist showed where there should have been the moon; the sleep-locked sea of the bay sighed. A smell of fern-rot and sea-water and gravel passed by Teresa into the house. Frank came to the hall door and saw her in the mist close to the car. He thought, calmly, of Linda wondering where he was, and wanted to go, and wanted to stay, and conceived how foolish it was, in love, to have to differentiate between women. In love there is no right and wrong, only the wish. However, he left Teresa alone and, going back into the drawing-room, said something further to Clifford about dinner.

Mrs. Massey was just detaching her arms from Clifford's neck. 'I had to kiss him,' she said. 'He'll never understand why.' She went slowly ahead of the two men out to the car. 'Dinner?' she said. 'Is that really what time it is? . . . Teresa?'

But there was no reply.

Up the mist between the formless rhododendrons the Alvis, with Frank and Clifford, crawled back to the main road. 'If you thought of turning this car in before leaving this country,' Frank said, 'you might let me know first? My name's Mull – Mull, Cork always finds me.'

'My name is Perry-Dunton,' said Clifford, after a pause.

'Yes, I thought it might be.'

'Why?' said Clifford, alarmed.

'Caught my eye on the register. You two seem to like it here. And how right you are. Staying on?'

'Well, we're not quite sure of our plans.'

'I wish I wasn't – we've only got the week-end. Look, why don't you two drop down for a drink with us after dinner? My cousin would be delighted.'

'It is most awfully nice of you, but I don't think——'

'Right-o,' said Frank, nodding his head.

LOOK AT ALL THOSE ROSES

Lou exclaimed at that glimpse of a house in a sheath of startling flowers. She twisted round, to look back, in the open car, till the next corner had cut it out of sight. To reach the corner, it struck her, Edward accelerated, as though he were jealous of the rosy house – a house with gables, flat-fronted, whose dark windows stared with no expression through the flowers. The garden, with its silent, burning gaiety, stayed in both their minds like an apparition.

One of those conflicts between two silent moods had set up, with Lou and Edward, during that endless drive. Also, there is a point when an afternoon oppresses one with fatigue and a feeling of unreality. Relentless, pointless, unwinding summer country made nerves ache at the back of both their eyes. This was a late June Monday; they were doubling back to London through Suffolk by-roads, on the return from a week-end. Edward, who detested the main roads, had traced out their curious route before starting, and Lou now sat beside him with the map on her knees. They had to be back by eight, for Edward, who was a writer, to finish and post an article: apart from this, time was no object with them. They looked forward with no particular pleasure to London and unlocking the stuffy flat, taking in the milk, finding bills in the letter-box. In fact, they looked forward to nothing with particular pleasure. They were going home for the purely negative reason that there was nowhere else they could as cheaply go. The week-end had not been amusing, but at least it had been 'away'. Now they could foresee life for weeks ahead – until someone else invited them – the typewriter, the cocktail-shaker, the telephone, runs in the car out of London to nowhere special. Love when Edward got a cheque in the post, quarrels about people on the way home from parties – and Lou's anxiety always eating them. This future weighed on them like a dull burden . . . So they had been glad to extend today.

But under a vacant sky, not sunny but full of diffused glare, the drive had begun to last too long: they felt bound up in the tired impotence of a dream. The stretches of horizon were stupefying. The road bent round wedges of cornfield, blocky elms dark with summer: for these last ten miles the countryside looked abandoned; they passed dropping gates, rusty cattle-troughs and the thistly, tussocky, stale grass of neglected farms. There was nobody on the roads; perhaps there was nobody anywhere . . . In the heart of all this, the roses looked all the odder.

'They were extraordinary,' she said (when the first corner was turned) in her tired, little, dogmatic voice.

'All the more,' he agreed, 'when all the rest of the country looks something lived in by poor whites.'

'I wish we lived *there*,' she said. 'It really looked like somewhere.'

'It wouldn't if we did.'

Edward spoke with some tartness. He had found he had reason to dread week-ends away: they unsettled Lou and started up these fantasies. Himself, he had no illusions about life in the country: life without people was absolutely impossible. What would he and she do with nobody to talk to but each other? Already, they had not spoken for two hours. Lou saw life in terms of ideal moments. She found few ideal moments in their flat.

He went on: 'You know you can't stand ear-wigs. And we should spend our lives on the telephone.'

'About the earwigs?'

'No. About ourselves.'

Lou's smart little monkey face became dolorous. She never risked displeasing Edward too far, but she was just opening her mouth to risk one further remark when Edward jumped and frowned. A ghastly knocking had started. It seemed to come from everywhere, and at the same time to be a special attack on them. Then it had to be traced to the car's vitals: it jarred up Lou through the soles of her feet. Edward slowed to a crawl and stopped. He and she confronted each other with that completely dramatic lack of expression they kept for occasions when the car went wrong. They tried crawling on again, a few tentative yards: the knocking took up again with still greater fury.

'Sounds to me like a big end gone.'

'Oh my goodness,' she said.

All the same, she was truly glad to get out of the car. She stretched and stood waiting on the grass roadside while Edward made faces into the bonnet. Soon he flung round to ask what she would suggest doing: to his surprise (and annoyance) she had a plan ready. She would walk back to that house and ask if they had a telephone. If they had not, she would ask for a bicycle and bicycle to the place where the nearest garage was.

Edward snatched the map, but could not find where they were. Where they were seemed to be highly improbable. 'I expect you,' Lou said, 'would rather stay with the car.' 'No, I wouldn't,' said Edward, 'anybody can have it . . . You like to be sure where I am, don't you?' he added. He locked their few odd things up in the boot of the car with the suitcases, and they set off in silence. It was about a mile.

There stood the house, waiting. Why should a house wait? Most pretty scenes have something passive about them, but this looked like a trap baited with beauty, set ready to spring. It stood back from the road. Lou put her hand on the gate and, with a touch of bravado, the two filed up the paved path to the door. Each side of the path, hundreds of standard roses bloomed, over-charged with colour, as though this were their one hour. Crimson, coral, blue-pink, lemon and cold white, they disturbed with fragrance the dead air. In this spell-bound afternoon, with no shadows, the roses glared at the strangers, frighteningly bright. The face of the house was plastered with tea-roses: waxy cream when they opened but with vermilion buds.

The blistered door was propped open with a bizarre object, a lump of quartz. Indoors was the dark, cold-looking hall. When they had come to the door they found no bell or knocker: they could not think what to do. 'We had better cough,' Lou said. So they stood there coughing, till a door at the end of the hall opened and a lady or woman looked out – they were not sure which. 'Oh?' she said, with no expression at all.

'We couldn't find your bell.'

'There they are,' she said, pointing to two Swiss cow-bells that hung on loops of string by the door she had just come out of. Having put this right, she continued to look at them, and out through the door past them, wiping her powerful-looking hands vaguely against the sides of her blue overall. They could hardly see themselves as intruders when their intrusion made so little effect. The occupying inner life of this person was not for an instant suspended by their presence. She was a shabby amazon of a woman, with a sculptural clearness about the face. She must have lost contact with the outer world completely: there was now nothing to 'place' her by. It is outside attachments – hopes, claims, curiosities, desires, little touches of greed – that put a label on one to help strangers. As it was, they could not tell if she were rich or poor, stupid or clever, a spinster or a wife. She seemed prepared, not anxious, for them to speak. Lou, standing close beside Edward, gave him a dig in a rib. So Edward explained to the lady how they found themselves, and asked if she had a telephone or a bicycle.

She said she was sorry to say she had neither. Her maid had a bicycle, but had ridden home on it. 'Would you like some tea?' she said. 'I am just boiling the kettle. Then perhaps you can think of something to do.' This lack of grip of the crisis made Edward decide the woman must be a moron: annoyance contused his face. But Lou, who wanted tea and was attracted by calmness, was entirely won. She looked at Edward placatingly.

'Thank you,' he said. 'But I must do something at once. We haven't got all night; I've got to be back in London. Can you tell me where I can telephone from? I must get through to a garage – a good garage.'

Unmoved, the lady said: 'You'll have to walk to the village. It's about three miles away.' She gave unexpectedly clear directions, then looked at Lou again.

'Leave your wife here,' she said. 'Then she can have tea.'

Edward shrugged; Lou gave a brief, undecided sigh. How much she wanted to stop. But she never liked to be left. This partly arose from the fact that she was not Edward's wife: he was married to someone else and his wife would not divorce him. He might some day go back to her, if this ever became the way of least resistance. Or he might, if it were the way of even less resistance, move on to someone else. Lou was determined neither should ever happen. She did love Edward, but she also stuck to him largely out of contentiousness. She quite often asked herself why she did. It seemed important – she could not say why. She was determined to be a necessity. Therefore she seldom let him out of her sight – her idea of love was adhesiveness . . . Knowing this well, Edward gave her a slightly malign smile, said she had far better stay, turned, and walked down the path without her. Lou, like a lost cat, went half-way to the door. 'Your roses are wonderful . . .' she said, staring out with unhappy eyes.

'Yes, they grow well for us, Josephine likes to see them.' Her hostess added: 'My kettle will be boiling. Won't you wait in there?'

Lou went deeper into the house. She found herself in a long, low and narrow parlour, with a window at each end. Before she could turn round, she felt herself being looked at. A girl of about thirteen lay, flat as a board, in a wicker invalid carriage. The carriage was pulled out across the room, so that the girl could command the view from either window, the flat horizons that bounded either sky. Lying there with no pillow she had a stretched look. Lou stood some distance from the foot of the carriage: the dark eyes looked at her down thin cheekbones, intently. The girl had an unresigned, living face; one hand crept on the rug over her breast. Lou felt, here was the nerve and core of the house . . . The only movement was made by a canary, springing to and fro in its cage.

'Hullo,' Lou said, with that deferential smile with which one approaches an invalid. When the child did not answer, she went on: 'You must wonder who I am?'

'I don't now; I did when you drove past.'

'Then our car broke down.'

'I know, I wondered whether it might.'

Lou laughed and said: 'Then you put the evil eye on it.'

The child ignored this. She said: 'This is not the way to London.'

'All the same, that's where we're going.'

'You mean, where you were going . . . Is that your husband who has just gone away?'

'That's Edward: yes. To telephone. He'll be back.' Lou, who was wearing a summer suit, smart, now rather crumpled, of honey-yellow linen, felt Josephine look her up and down. 'Have you been to a party?' she said, 'or are you going to one?'

'We've just been staying away,' Lou walked nervously down the room to the front window. From here she saw the same roses Josephine saw: she thought they looked like forced roses, magnetized into being. Magnetized, buds uncurled and petals dropped. Lou began to wake from the dream of the afternoon: her will stirred; she wanted to go; she felt apprehensive, threatened. 'I expect you like to lie out of doors, with all those roses?' she said.

'No, not often: I don't care for the sky.'

'You just watch through the window?'

'Yes,' said the child, impatiently. She added: 'What are the parts of London with most traffic?'

'Piccadilly Circus. Trafalgar Square.'

'Oh, I would like to see those.'

The child's mother's step sounded on the hall flags: she came in with the tea-tray. 'Can I help you?' said Lou, glad of the interim.

'Oh, thank you. Perhaps you'd unfold that table. Put it over here beside Josephine. She's lying down because she hurt her back.'

'My back was hurt six years ago,' said Josephine. 'It was my father's doing.'

Her mother was busy lodging the edge of the tray on the edge of the tea-table.

'Awful for him,' Lou murmured, helping unstack the cups.

'No, it's not,' said Josephine. 'He has gone away.'

Lou saw why. A man in the wrong cannot live where there is no humanity. There are enormities you can only keep piling up. He had bolted off down that path, as Edward had just done. Men cannot live with sorrow, with women who embrace it. Men will suffer a certain look in animals' eyes, but not in women's eyes. And men dread obstinacy, of love, of grief. You could stay with burning Josephine, not with her mother's patient, exalted face . . . When her mother had gone again, to fetch the teapot and kettle, Josephine once more fastened her eyes on Lou. 'Perhaps your husband will be some time,' she said. 'You're the first new person I have seen for a year. Perhaps he will lose his way.'

'Oh, but then I should have to look for him!'

Josephine gave a fanatical smile. 'But when people

go away they sometimes quite go,' she said. 'If they always come back, then what is the good of moving?'

'I don't see the good of moving.'

'Then stay here.'

'People don't just go where they want; they go where they must.'

'Must you go back to London?'

'Oh, I have to, you know.'

'Why?'

Lou frowned and smiled in a portentous, grown-up way that meant nothing at all to either herself or Josephine. She felt for her cigarette case and, glumly, found it empty – Edward had walked away with the packet of cigarettes that he and she had been sharing that afternoon. He also carried any money she had.

'You don't know where he's gone to,' Josephine pointed out. 'If you had to stay, you would soon get used to it. We don't wonder where my father is.'

'What's your mother's name?'

'Mrs. Mather. She'd like you to stay. Nobody comes to see us; they used to, they don't now. So we only see each other. They may be frightened of something——'

Mrs. Mather came back, and Josephine looked out of the other window. This immediate silence marked a conspiracy, in which Lou had no willing part. While Mrs. Mather was putting down the teapot, Lou looked round the room, to make sure it was ordinary. This window-ended parlour was lined with objects that looked honest and worn without having antique grace. A faded room should look homely. But extinct paper and phantom cretonnes gave this a gutted air. Rooms can be whitened and gutted by too-intensive living, as they are by a fire. It was the garden, out there, that focused the senses. Lou indulged for a minute the astounding fancy that Mr. Mather lay at the roses' roots . . . Josephine said sharply: 'I don't want any tea,' which made Lou realize that she would have to be fed and did not want to be fed in front of the stranger Lou still was. Mrs. Mather made no comment: she drew two chairs to the table and invited Lou to sit down. 'It's rather sultry,' she said. 'I'm afraid your husband may not enjoy his walk.'

'How far did you say it was?'

'Three miles.'

Lou, keeping her wrist under the table, glanced down covertly at her watch.

'We are very much out of the way,' said Mrs. Mather.

'But perhaps you like that?'

'We are accustomed to quiet,' said Mrs. Mather, pouring out tea. 'This was a farm, you know. But it was an unlucky farm, so since my husband left I have let the land. Servants seem to find that the place is lonely – country girls are so different now. My present servant is not very clear in her mind, but she works well and does not seem to feel lonely. When she is not working she rides home.'

'Far?' said Lou, tensely.

'A good way,' said Mrs. Mather, looking out of the window at the horizon.

'Then aren't you rather . . . alone? – I mean, if anything happened.'

'Nothing more can happen,' said Mrs. Mather. 'And there are two of us. When I am working upstairs or am out with the chickens, I wear one of those bells you see in the hall, so Josephine can always hear where I am. And I leave the other bell on Josephine's carriage.

83

When I work in the garden she can see me, of course.'
She slit the wax-paper top off a jar of jam. 'This is my
last pot of last year's damson,' she said. 'Please try
some; I shall be making more soon. We have two fine
trees.'

'You should see mother climb them,' said Josephine.
'Aren't you afraid of falling?'

'Why?' said Mrs. Mather, advancing a plate of rather
rich bread and butter. 'I never eat tea, thank you,'
Lou said, sitting rigid, sipping round her cup of tea like
a bird.

'She thinks if she eats she may have to stay here for
ever,' Josephine said. Her mother, taking no notice,
spread jam on her bread and butter and started to eat in
a calmly voracious way. Lou kept clinking her spoon
against the teacup: every time she did this the canary
started and fluttered. Though she knew Edward could
not possibly come yet, Lou kept glancing down the
garden at the gate. Mrs. Mather, reaching out for more
bread and butter, saw, and thought Lou was looking at
the roses. 'Would you like to take some back to London?'
she said.

Josephine's carriage had been wheeled out on the
lawn between the rosebeds. She lay with eyes shut and
forehead contracted, for overhead hung the dreaded
space of the sky. But she had to be near Lou while Lou
cut the roses. In a day or two, Lou thought, I should be
wearing a bell. What shall I do with these if I never do
go? she thought, as she cut through the strong stems
between the thorns and piled the roses on the foot of the
carriage. I shall certainly never want to look at roses
again. By her wrist watch it was six o'clock – two hours

since Edward had started. All round, the country under the white, stretched sky was completely silent. She went once to the gate.

'Is there any way from that village?' she said at last. 'Any 'bus to anywhere else? Any taxi one could hire?'

'I don't know,' said Josephine.

'When does your servant come back?'

'Tomorrow morning. Sometimes our servants never come back at all.'

Lou shut the knife and said: 'Well, those are enough roses.' She supposed she could hear if whoever Edward sent for the car came to tow it away. The car, surely, Edward would not abandon? She went to the gate again. From behind her Josephine said: 'Then please wheel me indoors.'

'If you like. But I shall stay here.'

'Then I will. But please put something over my eyes.'

Lou got out her red silk handkerchief and laid this across Josephine's eyes. This made the mouth more revealing: she looked down at the small resolute smile. 'If you want to keep on listening,' the child said, 'you needn't talk to me. Lie down and let's pretend we're both asleep.'

Lou lay down on the dry, cropped grass alongside the wheels of the carriage: she crossed her hands under her head, shut her eyes and lay stretched, as rigid as Josephine. At first she was so nervous, she thought the lawn vibrated under her spine. Then slowly she relaxed. There is a moment when silence, no longer resisted, rushes into the mind. She let go, inch by inch, of life, that since she was a child she had been clutching so desperately – her obsessions about this and that, her obsession about keeping Edward. How anxiously she had run from place to place, wanting to keep everything inside her own power. I should have stayed still: I shall stay still now, she thought. What I want must come to me: I shall not go after it. People who stay still generate power. Josephine stores herself up, and so what she wants happens, because she knows what she wants. I only think I want things; I only think I want Edward. (He's not coming and I don't care, I don't care.) I feel life myself now. No wonder I've been tired, only half getting what I don't really want. Now I want nothing; I just want a white circle.

The white circle distended inside her eyelids and she looked into it in an ecstasy of indifference. She knew she was looking at nothing – then knew nothing. . . .

Josephine's voice, from up in the carriage, woke her. 'You were quite asleep.'

'Was I?'

'Take the handkerchief off: a motor's coming.'

Lou heard the vibration. She got up and uncovered Josephine's eyes. Then she went to the foot of the carriage and got her roses together. She was busy with this, standing with her back to the gate, when she heard the taxi pull up, then Edward's step on the path. The taxi driver sat staring at the roses. 'It's all right,' Edward shouted, 'they're sending out from the garage. They should be here any moment. But what people – God! – Look here, have you been all right?'

'Perfectly, I've been with Josephine.'

'Oh, hullo, Josephine,' Edward said, with a hasty exercise of his charm. 'Well, I've come for this woman. Thank you for keeping her.'

'It's quite all right, thank you . . . Shall you be going now?'

'We must get our stuff out of the car: it will have to be towed to the garage. Then when I've had another talk to the garage people we'll take this taxi on and pick up a train . . . Come on, Lou, come on! We don't want to miss those people! And we've got to get that stuff out of the car!'

'Is there such a hurry?' she said, putting down the roses.

'Of course, there's a hurry . . .' He added, to Josephine: 'We'll look in on our way to the station, when I've fixed up all this, to say goodbye to your mother.' He put his hand on Lou's shoulder and punted her ahead of him down the path. 'I'm glad you're all right,' he said, as they got into the taxi. 'You're well out of that, my girl. From what I heard in the village——'

'What, have you been anxious?' said Lou, curiously.

'It's a nervy day,' said Edward, with an uneasy laugh. 'And I had to put in an hour in the village emporium, first waiting for my call, then waiting for this taxi. (And this is going to cost us a pretty penny.) I got talking, naturally, one way and another. You've no idea what they said when they heard where I had parked you. Not a soul round there will go near the place. I must say – discounting gossip – there's a story there,' said Edward. 'They can't fix anything, but . . . Well, you see, it appears that this Mather woman . . .' Lowering his voice, so as not to be heard by the driver, Edward began to tell Lou what he had heard in the village about the abrupt disappearance of Mr. Mather.

ATTRACTIVE MODERN
HOMES

No sooner were the Watsons settled into their new home than Mrs. Watson was overcome by melancholy. The actual settling-in was over only too soon. They had bought the house before it was done building, which had meant putting in time in rooms nearby; she had looked forward to having her own things round her again, and come, perhaps, to expect too much of them. The day the last workman left, the Watsons took possession. He screwed the bronze name-plate on to the gate, while she immediately put up the orange curtains to give the façade style and keep strangers from looking in. But her things appeared uneasy in the new home. The armchairs and settee covered in jazz tapestry, the sideboard with mirror panel, the alabaster light bowls, even the wireless cabinet looked sulky, as though they would rather have stayed in the van. The semi-detached house was box-like, with thin walls: downstairs it had three rooms and a larder, upstairs, three rooms and a bath. The rooms still smelled of plaster, the bath of putty. The stairs shook when the wardrobe was carried up: the whole structure seemed to be very frail.

Shavings and trodden paper littered the unmade garden and a persistent hammering from unfinished houses travelled over the fence. Even after dark these hollow echoes continued, for Eagles, the builder, was selling houses as fast as he put them up, and his men worked overtime, hammering on in the raw brick shells by candlelight. Earthy emanations and smells of shavings, singing and the plonk of boards being dropped filled the autumn darkness on the estate. The gored earth round the buildings looked unfriendly with pain. Outside the gates, drain trenches had been filled in roughly, but the roads were not made yet – they were troughs of mud, harrowed by builders' lorries this wet autumn, and bounded only by kerbs, along which you picked your way. It would not be possible yet to get a car out.

The Watsons' house, which they had called Rhyll, stood at the far edge of the estate, facing a row of elms along a lane that used to be called Nut Lane. Between the trees, one hedge had been broken down, leaving a flank of the lane bare to the new road alongside the row of villa gates. The Watsons' best room windows stared between the trees at a field that rose beyond them: a characterless hill. Almost no one passed, and nobody looked in.

Mr. Watson considered the trees an advantage. He was quick to point out any advantage, with a view to cheering his wife up. His promotion in business, so querulously awaited, came hard on her now it had come, for it entailed a transfer to another branch of the firm and the move here from the place they had always known. Here they were utter strangers; they had not a soul to speak to; no one had heard of them. The eighty miles they had travelled might have been eight hundred. Where they came from they had been born: there had been his people and her people and the set they had grown up with. Everyone took them for granted and thought well of them, so their ten years of marriage had been rich with society. Mrs. Watson enjoyed society and esteem and was dependent upon them, as women naturally are. When she had heard they must move she had said at once: 'We might as well go straight to the Colonies,' though after that she enjoyed the melancholy importance the prospect of moving gave her among her friends. Yes, where they came from many people were sorry, if not seriously upset, when the Watsons left: they said it was too bad. But their having come here made no difference to anyone. No one remarked their curtains, no one glanced at their door.

This new town they had come to had a mellow, ancient core, but was rapidly spreading and filling up with workers. The Watsons had been edged out to this new estate, the only place where they could find a house. And how un-ideal it was. An estate is not like a village, it has no heart; even the shops are new and still finding their own feet. It has not had time to take on the prim geniality of a suburb. The dwellers are pioneers unennobled by danger. Everybody feels strange and has no time for curiosity. Nothing has had time to flower in this new place. .

For instance, the Watsons had neighbours – the houses on either side were already done and lived in. But it had struck her that when they were moving in – while their van stood at the gate and her imposing furniture jolted up the unmade path – not a next-door curtain twitched; nobody took note. No one asked her in for a cup of tea, that first day, or even offered a cup over the fence. Where she came from, it had been customary to do this for newcomers who had not yet unpacked the kettle.

'It seems odd to me,' she had remarked to her husband.

He had been glad to have no one coming around to stare. But he was sorry to have her taking against the neighbours, this would make for no good: 'They're newcomers themselves,' was all he could find to say.

'Then you would think they might think.'

He looked worried, and she mistook his expression for crossness. 'Oh, all right,' she said. 'I merely passed the remark. There's no harm in my passing a remark occasionally, I suppose.'

She had never needed imagination herself, but now felt for the first time its absence in other people. Soon she suspected everyone but herself to be without natural feeling. For instance, she had worked on the children's feelings about the move, pointing out that they were leaving their little friends for ever and that their grannies, who loved them, would now be far away. So that Freddie and Vera wept when they got into the train and whined a good deal during the time in rooms. But now they were delighted with their surroundings; they enjoyed squelching in the deep mud. The half-built houses with their skeleton roofs, scaffolding, tubs of mortar, stacks of piping, and salmon-pink window-frames magnetized Freddie, who wished to become a builder. Where they came from, everything had been complete for years. He explored the uphill reaches of Nut Lane where hedges still arched over to make a tunnel. Vera liked tossing her curls and showing off at her new school, where, her mother warned her, the children were common. Vera was a child with naturally nice ways who would throw anything off, but Mrs. Watson kept watching Freddie closely to see he did not pick his nose, drop 'h's or show any other signs of having been in bad company. There was only one school near here: they had no choice . . . Seeing the children's horrible good spirits, Mrs. Watson said to her husband, 'How children do forget!' Her manner to Freddie and Vera became reproachful and wan. The old gentleman in the house they were semi-detached from gave Vera a peppermint over the fence, but did not speak to her mother.

To realize one's unhappiness as a whole needs some largeness, even of an ignoble kind. Mrs. Watson pitched upon details. The estate was a mile and half out of the town and 'buses only ran every twenty minutes. By the time you got anywhere it was time to start home again. And what is the good of shops with nobody to walk round with? Also, back where they came from she was accustomed to have a girl in daily to work, but here there was no way of hearing of any girl, so she had to work alone. Being alone all day, she never heard any news except what was in the paper. Back where they came from hardly a morning passed without someone dropping in, or out shopping you met someone, or when you went down the road you knew from the look of windows that people knew Mrs. Watson was going by. Whatever she bought or did invited some heartfelt comment. And he and she had been often invited out. Here they did not even go to the movies; to leave the house after dark fell was not tempting, for lamps along the estate roads were few and dim, making it hard to pick your way on the kerb, and her dread of stepping into the deep mud became neurotic.

Mr. Watson had a vice: he was a reader. And he was also always happy messing about with the wireless. He was out all day and talked to men at the office. At week-ends he got on with making the garden; the children played up the lane and she spent most of Saturday wiping mud off the line. Once, after tea, Freddie came in with a white face to say he had seen something funny up Nut Lane. Though his mother told him at once not to be so naughty, this made her come over queerish, later, herself. She got to dread the country left dingily at their door.

Up to now she had been happy without knowing, like a fortunate sheep or cow always in the same field. She was a woman who did not picture herself. She had looked into mirrors only to pat her perm down or smooth a jumper nicely over her bust. Everything that had happened to her seemed natural – love, marriage, the birth of Freddie, then Vera – for she had seen it happen to someone else. She never needed to ask what was happening really. No wonder the move had been like stepping over a cliff. Now no one cared any more whether she existed; she came to ask, without words, if she did exist. Yes, she felt sure there *must* be a Mrs. Watson. Asking why she felt sure, she fell prey to every horror of the subjective world. Wandering, frightened, there, she observed with apathy that the perm was growing out of her hair; some days she never took off her overall. She fell into a way of standing opposite the mantel mirror in the front room on heavy afternoons. The room was made water-grey by the elms opposite, that had not yet shed their rotting autumn leaves – there was no frost, no wind, no reason why they should ever fall. There are no words for such dismay. Her blue eyes began to dilate oddly; her mouth took on an uncertain stubborn twist. The hammering from behind the house continued; now and then a gate down the road clicked and somebody walked past without knowing her.

In all Eagles' houses the married bedroom is at the front. At this time of year the sun rose behind the hill, casting shadows of elms across the blanket about the moment that Mrs. Watson woke. The orange curtains would flame, the bedroom dazzle with sunshine. Though rain often set in later and almost all nights were wet, the early mornings were brilliant. She used to sit up, pull off her shingle-cap and shake out her short, blonde hair, seeing light burn its tips. The empty promise of morning shot a pang through her heart to tell her she was awake again. Mr. Watson slept late with determination; you saw his dread of waking under his lids. He lay beside her in a pre-natal attitude, legs crossed and drawn up, one cheek thrust into the pillow. The ripple his wife's getting up sent across the mattress did not ever disturb him. When she had lit the geyser, set breakfast and started the children dressing she would come back and shake the end of the bed. The first thing he always saw was his wife at the bed's foot, gripping the brass with sun flaming round the tips of her hair. A Viking woman, foreign to all he knew of Muriel, with eyes remorseless as the remorseless new day, fixed on him a stare that he did not dare to plumb.

She had given up grumbling and seldom passed remarks now. Something behind her silence he learned to dread.

Saturdays were his half-days. One Saturday, when they had been there about eight weeks, he suddenly stuck his fork upright into the garden soil, eased the palms of his townish hands which had blistered, scraped off clods from his insteps on to the fork and went indoors to the kitchen to run the tap. He did all this in the decisive manner of someone acting on impulse, shy of

94

himself. Towelling his face and hands on the roller he instinctively listened. Rhyll was a sounding box and she could be heard not there. She did say something, he thought, about going into town. Freddie and Vera were out about the estate. So there was no one to wonder . . . So he stepped round the house and out at the front gate. Since they came, he had had no secret pleasure. Today he would start up Nut Lane which, unknown, edged the estate with savageness.

Standing between the stumps of broken-down hedges he looked back at their road. A single twist of smoke from a chimney melted into the thin November grey, but the houses with close 'art' curtains looking unliving – what should animate them? Behind, scaffolding poles, squares more of daylight being entombed there . . . Inside, the lane was full of builders' rubbish. He started uphill, stepping from rib to rib of slimy hardness over chasms of mud. Rotting leaves made silent whole reaches of lane. Recoiling from branches in the thickety darkness, he thought he had not asked what Freddie said he had seen. The idea of a ghost's persistent aliveness comforted some under part of his mind.

The slope slackened, the lane was running level through a scrubby hazel wood with the sky behind. This must be round the other side of the hill. He looked into the wood which, because he had not known it existed, looked as though no one had ever seen it before. Part of its strangeness was a woman's body face down on the ground. Her arms were stretched out and she wore a mackintosh. With a jump of vulgar excitement he wondered if she were dead. Then the fair hair unnaturally fallen forward and red belt of the mackintosh showed him this was his wife, who could not be dead. Her manner of being here made his heart stop; then he felt hot colour come up his neck. He foresaw her shame at lying like this here; having heard steps she was keeping her face hidden. He could not have been more stricken in his idea of her if he had found her here with another man. He did not like to see her embrace the earth.

Waiting to bolt if she stirred, he stood where he was, eyeing her figure; its fiercely abject line. He stepped sharply up the bank into the wood. Her not stiffening as he approached shocked him. He pulled up and saw her contract one hand.

He heard himself say: 'So you didn't go to town?'

'No.'

'Feeling bad?'

'I'm all right.'

'Then look here,' he said, his voice humping a tone, 'you oughtn't to be like that in a place like this. I might have been anyone.'

'What of it?' she said, her mouth muffled by grass.

'Besides, look here . . . That grass is reeking wet.'

'That's up to me,' she said. 'Get out. Why keep on coming after me?'

'How should I know? I was simply taking a turn.'

'Well, take your turn,' said her dead voice.

He took an angry forward step, looking down at her violently. Nothing appears more wanton than despair. 'I won't have it,' he said, 'it isn't decent. Get up.'

She drew her arms in, pushed herself on to her knees and got right up in one slow, disdainful movement, keeping her face away. 'Decent?' she said. 'This place isn't anywhere.'

'It's round where we live.'

'Live?' she said, 'What do you mean, live?'

'Well, we——'

'What do you mean, we?'

'You and I,' he said, looking sideways at her shoulder.

'Yes,' she said. 'It's fine for me having you. Sometimes anyone would almost think you could speak.'

'Well, what is there to say?'

'Don't ask me.'

'Well, you've got a home.'

'Oh, yes,' she said, 'I have, haven't I? Yes, it's sweet, isn't it? Like you see in advertisements.' She thrust her thumbs under the belt of her mackintosh.

'You've no business . . .' he said. 'Suppose Freddie or Vee had happened to come up here. That'd have been a nice . . .'

'Well, it'd show Vera . . .'

'Look here,' he said, 'You're batty!'

'No; I'm just noticing.'

Catching at her near shoulder he pulled her round to face him. His excitement, unfamiliar, excited him; he saw his rage tower. She stood stock still in her buttoned mackintosh, staring woodenly past his shoulder at the bleak wood, unconscious as any dummy of being touched. She said: 'Why is it awful?'

'It's a new place.'

'Yes. But it oughtn't to be awful, not awful like this.'

'Awful?'

'You know it is.'

'We've got each other.'

She gave him that glazed, unironic, really terrible look. Throat nervously filling up, he objected again – 'But, people . . .'

'Yes, I know they do. Even right in the country

miles off. They seem to get on all right. So what I want to know is. . .'

'You expect such a whole lot. . . .'

'No. Only what's natural.'

He frowned down at the form she had left in the crushed, autumny grass for so long that she looked down at it too. 'There must be some way,' he said. 'To keep going, I mean.'

'Yes, there ought to be,' she said. 'If you ask me, I don't know what a house like that is meant for. You can't think what it's like when you're in it the whole time. I can't understand, really.'

'We're the same as we've been always.'

'Yes,' she said, 'but it didn't notice before.'

He changed colour and said, 'You know I . . . I think the world of you.'

'Well, you've sort of got to, haven't you?' she replied unmovedly. 'Why aren't the two of us having a better time?'

'Well, we don't know anyone yet.'

'I wonder,' she said. 'Do you think there's so much in that?'

He looked at the wood's dead glades and emasculate, sparse leaves thin with afternoon light. 'You know,' he said, 'this place will be nice in spring. We might come here quite a lot.'

But, not listening, she said, 'The way we live, we never know anyone. All that crowd back at home, they've forgotten us. It was all coming in for coffee, or else whist. It doesn't get you anywhere. I mean, you get used to it, but that doesn't make it natural. What I mean is. . . .'

However, she broke off there and began to walk away,

stepping down the low bank into the lane. 'Yes,' she said in a different voice, 'it's a nice wood. The kids know it quite well.'

'What d'you think Freddie saw?' he said rapidly, following her downhill.

'Oh, I don't know. I daresay he saw himself.' Tilted on wobbling heels she went downhill ahead of him, low branches thwacking against the thighs of her mackintosh. A crimpled dead leaf caught in her hair, over her turned-up collar. He followed, eyes on the leaf, doggedly striding, stumbling between the ruts. It was going on tea-time: in the tunnel of lane the twilight was pretty deep and a dull, lightish glimmer came from her mackintosh. Coming down, the lane was shorter; the wood was near their door, too near their door.

When, one behind the other, they stepped through the broken hedge opposite Rhyll, a youngish woman stood at Rhyll gate, at a loss, looking about. She was hatless and wore a brick woollen three-piece suit. Her air was neighbourly.

She said, 'Oh, Mrs. Watson?'

Mrs. Watson replied guardedly.

'I hope I may introduce myself. I am Mrs. Dawkins from just along there. Kosy Kot. I was sorry to find you out. I am sure you won't mind my taking the liberty, but your Vera and my Dorothy have been playing together recently and I called in to ask if you'd think of kindly allowing Vera to stop to tea with Dorothy this afternoon. Mr. Dawkins and I would be most glad that she should.'

'Well, really, that's most kind of you, I'm sure. If Vera's a good girl, and comes home at half-past six. . . .'

'I did hope you would not think it a liberty, I have to

be careful with Dorothy, as we are quite newcomers, but Vera is such a sweet, nice little thing – I understand that you are newcomers also?'

'So to speak,' said Mrs. Watson. 'We've lived here about eight weeks. But the newer houses are lived in now, I see.'

'It's a nice estate,' said Mrs. Dawkins, 'isn't it? Convenient and yet in a way countrified. I shall be glad when they make the roads up; at present Mr. Dawkins cannot get his car out, which is disappointing for him.' She glanced at the blank beside Rhyll where there could be a baby garage.

'We've delayed getting our car till the roads were made,' said Mrs. Watson at once. 'The 'buses being so frequent and everything.'

Mr. Watson, looking surprised, edged past them in at Rhyll gate. Both ladies turned to watched him up to the path.

'I always say,' continued Mrs. Dawkins, 'that it takes time to settle into a place. Gentlemen, being out so much, don't feel it the same way.'

'It's hardly to be expected,' said Mrs. Watson. Putting a hand up to pat all round the shingle, she plucked the leaf from her hair. 'Still, I've no doubt a place grows on one. It's really all habit, isn't it?'

THE EASTER EGG PARTY

Their object was to restore her childhood to her. They were simple and zealous women, of an integrity rooted in flawless sentiment; they bowed to nothing but their own noble ideas, and flinched from nothing but abandoning these. They issued the invitation on an impulse but awaited the answer with no drop in morale. They did not shrink from facts, for they attended committees for the good of the world – most facts, however, got to West Wallows a little bit watered down: such things did happen, but not to people one knew. So that when their eye was drawn – they were unmarried sisters, with everything in common, and had, in regard to some things, one eye between them – when their eye was drawn by a once-quite-familiar name to an obscure paragraph in their daily paper, their hearts (or their heart) stopped. The case was given in outline, with unusual reticence. When they saw what had either happened or nearly happened – they were not quite clear which – to the little girl of a friend they had known as a little girl, shyness and horror drove a wedge between them; they became two people whose looks could not quite meet. Across the breakfast table of their large cottage, in the half-acre of garden already gladey and glittering with the first greens of spring, they failed to discuss the matter. After a day of solitary

side-by-side reflection it came up with them in its happier
practical aspect: 'Could one *do* anything now? . . . Is
there any way one could help?'

Eunice and Isabelle Evers were both just over fifty:
their unperplexed lives showed in their faces, lined only
by humour, and in their frank, high foreheads. They
were Amazons in homespuns, Amazons, without a touch
of deprivation or pathos; their lives had been one long
vigorous walk. Like successful nuns, they both had a
slightly married air. An unusual number of people in
Gloucestershire knew and respected them, and they cut
ice in the village of West Wallows. They thought the
world of children, of any children; and children, in
consequence, thought the world of them: they were past
mistresses at blowing that bubble world that is blown
for children by children-loving grown-ups – perhaps,
also the dearest of their own pleasures lay there. If
they had any fantasies, these centred round ponies and
bread-and-jam on the beach, and they still received
intimations of immortality.

Therefore, any unspeakable thing happening to any
child was more upsetting to them than if they had been
mothers. It was against their natures to judge Dorothea
(the friend they had known as a little girl) in any way.
All the same, across what line, into what world had she
wandered in these years since her marriage, since they
had lost sight of her, that her little girl should be exposed
to such things as this? Dorothea's marriage had failed.
Must one own she failed as a mother? They knew,
vaguely, Dorothea was 'on the stage' – though one never
saw her name on the programme of any play.

Dorothea's answer to their invitation took so long in
coming that they had begun to fear she was out of reach.

But when she did answer, Dorothea accepted with alacrity. She said that it really was truly sweet of them, and she only hoped they would find Hermione good. 'She's really as good as gold, but she's always rather reserved. I am sure it might do her good to be away from me for a bit; you see, I am really very upset these days. I suppose that's only natural; my nerves have always been awful, and now *this* coming, on top of everything else. It's nearly killed me, of course. I suppose one will get over it. Well, it really is dear of you; you always were such dears. *Oh*, how far away all those happy days seem now! . . . I will send Hermione down on April 12th. Yes, I think she's fond of animals; at all events you could try. Of course she's never had any, poor little soul.'

So they began to prepare for Hermione.

West Wallows was more than a village: it was a neighbourhood. From the wide street branched roads that led past the white gates of many homes. The rector was tactful and energetic, the squire unusually cultivated; there were a number of moderate-sized dwellings – some antique, some quite recently built. Inexpensive sociability, liberal politics, shapely antique family furniture, 'interests', enlightened charity set the note of the place. No one was very rich; nobody was eccentric, and, though few people hunted, nobody wrote letters against blood sports. The local families harmonized with the pleasant retired people who had settled here. Probably few neighbourhoods in England have such a nice atmosphere as West Wallows. In the holidays all the children had a jolly time . . . The Easter holidays were in progress now, and this created a slight predicament: how much should Hermione be with other children?

The Misses Evers decided to wait and see.

They decided to wait for grace and see what line things took. They hinted at nothing to anyone. In the week before Hermione came, the tortoiseshell cat Barbara was persuaded to wean her two patchy kittens, who learnt to lap prettily from an Umbrian saucer. The honeysuckle up the south front of the cottage unfolded the last of its green shoots, and in the garden and in the strip of orchard the other side of the brook daffodils blew their trumpets.

The first afternoon was windy. Every time a sucker of honeysuckle swung loose and tapped the window Hermione jumped. This was the only sign she gave of having grown-up nerves. She was not quite a pretty child; her face was a long, plump oval; her large dark-grey eyes were set rather close together, which gave her an urgent air. Her naturally curly dark hair had grown too long for a bob and swung just clear of her shoulders. She sat in the dark glass dome of her own inside world, just too composedly eating bread and honey. Now and then she glanced, with mysterious satisfaction, at the bangles on one or the other of her wrists.

'This is honey from our own bees, Hermione.'

'Goodness.'

'It tastes quite different from other honey, we think.'

'Yes; Mummy said you kept bees. Do you keep doves too?'

Eunice glanced at the white forms that whirled rather frighteningly over the wind-teased garden. 'Those are the next-door pigeons; they keep on flying over, so we have the fun of them.'

'The next-door cat in London keeps getting into our larder. I do hate cats.'

'Oh, but you must like Barbara – and she's got two kittens.'

'Cats always do that, don't they?'

After tea Eunice took her up to what was to be her room, the spare-room over the porch, snug as a ship's cabin and frilly with sprigged stuff. She showed her the sampler worked by another little girl of eleven, just a hundred years ago, and some framed photographs of Italy. 'That's Assisi, where St. Francis lived.'

'Goodness,' said Hermione, biting her thumb vaguely. She looked through the loops of dotted muslin curtain at the tops of the apple trees. 'It's just like on a calendar,' she said. She sat on the bed, with her tongue feeling round one cheek, while Eunice unpacked her two suit-cases for her. 'Oh, what pretty clothes and things,' said Eunice depracatingly. 'But I don't think you'll have a chance to wear most of them here. You'll want to wear old clothes and simply tumble about.'

'I haven't got any old clothes. Mummie gives them away.'

In her tweed skirt, with her knotted oak walking-stick, lifting her forehead to the sweet spring air Isabelle, next morning, swung down the village street, and Hermione walked beside her, changing step now and then with a queer little dancing hop. In her raspberry-woollen dress, her turned-up hat with the Donald Duck clip and her long, white, carefully pulled-up socks, the child looked like a stage child half-way through a tour: nothing would tone her down. Isabelle pointed out the village pond with its white ducks, the saddle-back church tower, the Beacon on the top of the steep, green, nursery-rhyme hill, the quaint old sign of the Spotted Cow, which made all children laugh – Hermione did not smile. A street is a street, and the point of a street is, people: looking boldly up, she challenged whoever passed with her dusky, gelatinous dark-grey eyes. It was their attention she wanted; she collected attention like twists of silver paper or small white pebbles. Her search for attention was so arduous that she gave less than half her mind to whatever Isabelle said. Whenever Isabelle turned into a shop, Hermione would ferret along the counter. In the chemist's she said she would like to buy that green celluloid box to keep her toothbrush in.

'Have you brought your pocket-money?' said Isabelle brightly.

'Oh – but I haven't any.'

'Then I'm afraid the green box will have to wait,' said Isabelle still more brightly, with an inspiring smile. She did not approve of buying hearts with small gifts: besides, one must teach Hermione not to 'hint'. Hermione gave the green box a last look, the first fully human look she had spent on anything since she came to West Wallows. She slowly dragged her eyes from it and followed Isabelle out of the chemist's shop.

'This afternoon,' said Isabelle, 'we'll go primrosing.'

'I think those lambs are pretty,' said Hermione, suddenly pointing over a wall. 'I should like a pet lamb of my own; I should call it Percy.'

'Well, perhaps you can make a friend of one of these lambs. If you go every day very quietly into the field——'

'But I want it to be my own; I want to call it Percy.'

'Well, let's call "Percy", and see which of them comes . . . Percy, Percy, Percy!' called Isabelle, leaning over the wall. None of the lambs took any notice: one of the sheep gave her a long, reproving look. Hermione, meanwhile, had frigidly walked away.

Eunice and Isabelle took it in turns to what they called take Hermione out of herself. They did not confess how unnerved they sometimes were by their sense of intense attention being focused on nothing. They took her in to see the neighbour who kept the pigeons; Eunice taught her to climb the safe apple trees; Isabelle took her out in a pair of bloomers and dared her to jump the brook. Hermione jumped in and was pulled out patient and very wet. They borrowed a donkey for her, and the run of a paddock, but she fell off the donkey three times. This child stayed alone the whole time and yet was never alone; their benevolent spying on her, down the orchard or through windows, always showed them the same thing – Hermione twirling round her silver bangles at some unseen person, or else tossing her hair. They took her primrosing three times; then they took her bird's-nesting in the Hall grounds. In the great hollow beech hedges, in the dense ivy, the secret nests excited her: she stood up on tiptoes; her cheeks flamed. But all this waned when she might not touch the eggs. She could not understand why. The glossy blues, the faint greens, the waxy buff-pinks, the freckles seemed to her to be for nothing: while the sisters, breathless, held apart the branches she now looked only glumly into the nests. When they found a brood of fledglings she ran six yards back and said: 'Ugh! Fancy leaving eggs just for *that*!'

'But they're alive, dear. Next Spring they'll be singing away, like all the birds we hear now, or laying eggs of their own.'

'Well, I don't see why.'

The sisters bound each other to silence with quick glances.

Hermione said: 'I'd sooner have sugar eggs.'

It was from this rather baffling afternoon that the idea of the Easter egg party arose.

Hermione ought now, they felt, if ever, to be fit for younger society. Perhaps she might find friends – how they doubted this! At all events, one must see. And since she was to meet children, why should she not meet all the West Wallows children at once? About a quite large party there should be something kind and ambiguous: if she failed to hit it off with Maisie or Emmeline, she might hit it off with Harriet or Joanna. (The fact was, they felt, in a way they rather dreaded to face, that in a large party she would stand out less.) The Misses Evers were well known for their juvenile parties, but up to now these had always been held at Christmas, when guessing games could be played, or at Midsummer, when they got permission for their young guests to help to make someone's hay. An Easter party was quite a new idea and looked like running them in for more expense – they did not jib at this, but they dreaded the ostentation. Isabelle bicycled into Market Chopping and bought three dozen sweet eggs – a little reduced in price, as Easter was just over. Some were chocolate, wrapped in brilliant metallic paper; some were marzipan, with the most naturalistic freckles; some were cardboard, containing very small toys. That same afternoon, Eunice, at her bureau, wrote out invitations to the fourteen young guests, ranging in age from fourteen down to six. As she addressed each envelope she would pause, to give Hermione, entrancedly doing nothing on the sofa beside her, a biography of each possible child.

The afternoon of the party was, happily, very fine. From three o'clock on the garden gate clicked incessantly: unaccompanied by grown-ups the guests in their coloured jerseys or very clean blouses came up the path – to be mustered by Eunice and Isabelle on the patch of lawn by the sundial. They were already tanned or freckled by the spring sun, and all wore an air of stolid elation. 'Now, finding *ought* to be keeping,' said Isabelle, 'but we think that if any one of you people finds more than three, he or she might hand the rest back, to go at the end to some other person who may not have been so clever.'

Eunice put in: 'And we shall be giving a prize: this Easter rabbit' (she held up a china ornament) 'to whoever hands in most eggs by the end of the afternoon.'

Isabelle took up: 'They are hidden about the garden and in the orchard the other side of the stream. To make things just a little easier we have tied a piece of pink wool *somewhere near* every place where an egg is. And whoever finds each egg must untie the pink wool, please, or it will be so difficult. Now, are we all here? Oh, no: we are still waiting for Poppy. The moment she's here I'm going to blow this whistle, then – off with you all! At five o'clock I shall blow the whistle for tea.'

At this moment the late-comer bolted in at the gate, whereupon Isabelle blew the whistle piercingly. The children – the boys were small, the girls larger-sized, some of them quite lumpy – glanced at each other, tittered and moved off. For some distance they stayed in compact formation, like explorers advancing in dangerous territory; though all the time their sharp eyes were glancing left and right. Then, in the glittering sunshine of the garden, shreds of pink wool began to be discerned. One by one children bounded off from the others, glancing jealously round to see that no one was on their tracks.

Hermione had lagged a little behind the party that moved off. She had been introduced to all the children by name, but after the 'how-d'you-do's no one had spoken to her. She had secured by the wrist the only other child that tagged behind the party, a small, dumb little boy: she gripped this child by the wrist as though he were not human – he appeared in some way to give her countenance. From the beginning she had been difficult: she had been reluctant to come down from her room at all: from the lawn below Eunice had called and waved; Hermione had answered but not come. Ghostly just inside her shut window, or like a paper figure pasted against the glass, she had watched strange children invade the garden she knew. She had gone on like a kitten that somehow gets up a tree, panics, and cannot be got down again – till Eunice ran up to dislodge her with some well-chosen words. But alas, once one had got her on to the lawn, her up-a-tree air only became more noticeable. She shook hands with a rigid arm, on which all the bracelets jumped. She looked straight at everyone, but from a moody height: what was evident was not just fear or shyness but a desperate, cut-off haughtiness. In her eyes existed a world of alien experi-ence. The jolly, tallish girls with their chubbed hair, the straddling little boys with their bare knees, apt to frown at the grass between their sandshoes, rebounded from that imperious stare. Either she cared too much or she did not care a fig for them – and in either case they did not know how to meet her.

Sloping south to the brook, the garden was made devious by swastika hedges: it was all grots and plots. Japanese plums caught light in their ethereal petals; flowering currants sent out their sweet, hot smell. The waving shreds of pink wool made round themselves centres of magnetic attraction in which children hummed and jostled, like the bees round the currants. The garden, the orchard became tense with the search: now and then yelps of triumph struck their silence like sharp bells. By the end of a half-hour everyone seemed to have found at least one egg. Children met to compare their spoils, then pounced jealously off again.

Only Hermione and the doomed little boy that she would not let go of had not yet found an egg. She sometimes shifted her grip on his hot wrist. In her haze of self-consciousness, weighted by that deep-down pre-occupation, she moved too slowly, dragging the little boy. Once or twice she did see pink wool, but when she got to the spot it was always being untied by the child who had found the egg. Disgraced by their failure, she and the little boy said not a word to each other; they moved about in a silence of deepening animosity. Now they stood on the bridge, between the garden and orchard: Hermione looked from one shore to the other with eyes that held incredulity and despair. She had not found *any* egg.

Without warning the little boy went rigid all over, braced himself against the rail of the bridge, threw open his cave of a mouth and yelled: 'Oh *Mais-see*, I wanner go with you!'

A girl bustling contentedly through the orchard,

three bright eggs shining on the palm of her hand, stopped and lifted her nose like a mother dog. Then she approached the bridge. 'I say,' she said to Hermione, 'would you mind letting my little brother go? He'd like to look by himself.'

'He and I are looking together.'

'Oh. How many have you each found?'

'Somebody else always finds the ones we are looking for.'

'Good gracious,' said Maisie, 'then haven't you found *any*? Someone says that Harriet's got six, and everyone else here has found at least two. Do you mean to say poor Simon hasn't got *any*? . . . Never mind, Simon; come and look with me. *We'll* soon find some.'

'I don't see why he should. Why should I be the only person left who hasn't got any egg?'

'Well, I can't help that, can I? You'd better look more properly . . . Come along, Simon.'

Hermione let him go.

When she found herself quite alone on the bridge she shaded her eyes (because the sun was descending) to peer at the round, white object under one apple tree. It was a panama hat, last seen on the girl Harriet: now it sat on the grass. As though something inside her answered a magnet, Hermione left the bridge and ran to that apple tree. The general search had ebbed back to the garden: in the orchard no one shouted; no one swished through the long grass – the place was deserted suddenly. Hermione knelt down, cautiously raised the hat, and saw the clutch of six supernatural eggs – two gold, one red, one silver and two blue. They lay tilted together in their nest in the grass. Trembling with satisfaction, she regarded them steadily. Then she made a pouch of her skirt and gathered the eggs up into it. Clumsily, cautiously rising, she made off at a trot for a hedge that cut off the orchard from Church Lane.

She was not missed till the five o'clock whistle sounded and the children trooped in through the french window for tea. Then Eunice and Isabelle combined to pass the contretemps over as smoothly as possible. While Eunice poured out, and kept the chatter going, Isabelle, with the whistle, slipped out for a thorough look. Sadly, sadly, she saw some trampled daffodils – the nicer the set of children, the larger their feet. When she got to the end of the orchard she saw the gap forced through the hedge, and her heart sank.

The big scandal only broke at the end of tea-time, when Eunice began to check up the eggs found. Throughout tea the outraged Harriet had not suffered in silence: there had been a good deal of mumbling at her end of the table, but Eunice did not know what the matter was. When the loss came out Eunice put two and two together with disheartening rapidity – so did every-one else. Speaking looks were cast by the West Wallows children at the place where Hermione did not sit. There was nothing for it but to present the china rabbit to Harriet with as much haste, and still as much pomp, as possible and to suggest we should now all play prisoners' base on the lawn.

Seven strokes from the church clock fell on the sad, clear evening. The Easter egg party guests had been sent home an hour ago; the sisters had returned from their desperate search up and down the village, in the fields, in the near woods. Something made Eunice go up to Hermione's room – there *was* Hermione, sitting on the bed. She must have slipped back while nobody was about. In the deep dusk she was sitting across the bed, legs stuck out and back stuck to the wall, in the attitude in which one props up a doll. She was, presumably, waiting: the moment the door opened, she said, without looking up: 'I want to go home now.'

'But Hermione——'

'Mummy said I needn't stay if I didn't like it. She said I could come straight home.'

'Dear, this isn't because you think *we* are . . . upset about anything?'

'I can't help *what* you are,' said Hermione, quite dispassionate. 'Couldn't you get some other girl to stay with you? There's nothing for me to do here; I mean, I can't do anything. And all those girls were awful to me today; nobody cared if I found an egg or not. That girl Maisie wouldn't let me play with her brother. No one has ever been so awful to me as they all were; they took all the eggs, and I never found even one. And you never let me talk, all the time, you never let me touch anything. You keep on making me take an interest in things, and you never take the slightest interest in me. Mummy said you were interested in me, but now I don't believe her. I feel just as if I was dead, and I do want to go home. Oh, and I took those six old eggs.'

'Well, hush now, dear: we're all tired. Hop into bed, like a good girl, and I'll bring you some biscuits and milk. Would you like me to bring up one of the kittens too?'

'No, thank you; your kittens scratch. Well, can I go home tomorrow?'

'We'll see about that tomorrow.'

Eunice sighed and went downstairs. She filled a beaker with milk and put out a plate of biscuits, then she looked into the parlour for a word with Isabelle.

The lamps were lit, but the curtains were not drawn yet: outside there was a dark twitter of birds. Isabelle, reading the look on her sister's face, came round the table, saying: 'Oh, Eunice. . . .'

'I know,' Eunice said. 'It apparently can't be helped. Her mind's set now on going home. I wonder whether she'd better . . .'

'Eunice, that's not like you!' cried Isabelle, with a burst of their old heroic energy.

'I know,' said Eunice, putting down the biscuits. Absently, she began to sip the milk. 'But you see, this is really not like anything else. There are times when being like one's self, however much one's self, does not seem much help. Well, there it is, Isabelle. We've always known life was difficult, but I must confess, till today I'd never really believed it. I don't see quite where we failed: she *is* a child, after all.'

'I suppose, once a child has been the centre of things . . .'

'Oh, look – I'm drinking this milk. It really was for Hermione.'

Hermione left next day: perhaps it was for the best. They never speak of her to the children at West Wallows, and the West Wallows children do not ask about her. The sisters seldom speak of her even between themselves; she has left a sort of scar, like a flattened grave, in their hearts. It rained the day she left, but cleared up again at sunset. When Isabelle, in her gum-boots, walking in the orchard, found the six Easter eggs under the original apple tree, the chocolate under the paper had gone to a pulp, and the gold and colours of the paper had run.

LOVE

IT was a funny experience, it was really – not like a thing that happened, more like a dream. Sometimes I think I did dream it – for all I can get out of Edna, I might have done. It's like Edna to put the whole thing on me – she does that by keeping on saying nothing. So of course I can never refer to it. And I don't know that I want to – not to Edna. Anyhow, Edna's shut up, just like a clam.

The minute we came round the rocks into that bay I felt there was something ... The day, with that sea glare and at the same time no sun, made everything look unnatural, and we were dead beat. We'd kept slogging along in that loose sand: our shoes were full of it. For miles we hadn't seen anything you could call anything – only rocks, and slopes coming down, and the same sea. So when we came round that rock and saw the hotel, it gave us quite a shock. The bay was ever so narrow, it looked private; the hotel stood back but sand came right up to it. There was a sort of jetty, but that had rotted. The hotel must have been pink, with a name painted across it, but the name and the colour had faded right out. All the shutters were up, but for one window: it looked like a dead person winking at you. I never did like being stared at. I said, 'Why, Edna, it's shut up.'

She said, 'Well, it *is* a poor-looking place!'

The hotel (I can see it now) had only two storeys, but it was quite long. And at one side they'd tacked on a sort of a wooden annexe, maybe for a dance-hall or restaurant. That was all shuttered up, too, inside the coloured glass. Along the front of it, though, went a great iron veranda, that looked as though it had come from some other place. Quite massive, it was, all pillars and scrolls and lace-work: it looked heavy enough to pull the whole annexe down. There were great steps, with the bottom buried in sand. What drew *my* eye to it was the bright blue dress of the lady sitting up there. She was not the sort of person you'd see anywhere. She sat up there, simply looking at us.

So Edna, to show she was within her rights, bumped down there on the sand and took her shoes off and shook all the sand out of them, one after the other. 'That's better,' she said. 'Why don't you? Go on,' but somehow I didn't like to. 'You are a silly,' she said. 'It's only just an hotel!'

I looked sideways and saw a board with 'Luncheons, Teas, Suppers', stuck there in the sand – but the writing ever so faint. 'I daresay it's all right,' I said. 'We might have come for our teas.'

'You and your tea,' she said. 'You're always on about tea.'

But I saw she wanted her tea as much as I did, from the way she whacked the sand out of her skirt. You can't help getting to notice a person's character when you work in the same office and go on holidays with them. If you asked me how I liked Edna I wouldn't know how to answer, but a girl on her own like I am has to put up with some things, and it's slow to go on your holiday all alone. I wouldn't mind keeping on noticing Edna's

character if she wouldn't keep on saying she keeps on
noticing mine. Still, we'd booked our room, so we had
to get along somehow – and it was only the fortnight,
after all. You get better value for money in quiet places,
so she and I had picked on a quiet place. Edna and I
aren't like some other girls in business, always off where
you can pick up a boy. For one thing, Edna hasn't got
much appeal – and I always was one to keep myself to
myself. It was quite a nice place Edna and I had picked
on, it was refined – but I must say it was a bit slow. No
other place up or down the coast for ever so many miles;
we really did ought to have brought bikes. We sun-
bathed a bit, but we somehow only burned red. It was
nice, safe bathing, but when it was cold for that, or too
windy for deck-chairs, there was nothing to do but go a
trudge on the sands. That suited Edna all right – she
always was quite a hiker – and I didn't like to be left.
We never walked much inland, as you'll understand,
because of the awful cows. I often said I did wish the
sand wasn't so soft, and Edna'd say, 'Whatever do you
expect?'

This day I'm talking about was the last day but one
of our holiday – that may have been the reason that,
once we'd started off walking, we'd come further along
than we ever had. I'd been wanting my tea some time,
though I wasn't going to say so, to make Edna start
picking at me.

'I doubt they serve teas,' I said. 'The place looks shut
up, to me.' 'Then what they want to leave that board
for?' said Edna. 'If they say teas, they've got to serve
teas.' She got quite red. 'Besides, look,' she said, sort of
spying at the veranda, 'besides, look; they've got a
visitor there.' So she started marching towards the

place. I went too – though it somehow didn't seem right.

The person on the veranda sat as still as an image. Only her eyes kept moving, following us. She let us come on till we were near up, then said, 'Oh, no, you mustn't go in!'

I must say Edna did jump, too, but she said, 'Well, this is an hotel all right, isn't it?'

The person looked sort of puzzled: she just said, 'You mustn't; they wouldn't like you to.'

'What are you up to, then?' said Edna, ever so sharp.

That gave the lady even more of a puzzle. Then she said, 'But I always sit outside.'

Being interfered with settled the thing for Edna; she just gave my elbow a sort of pull, and we walked away from the lady, past all those shut shutters, round the end of the hotel. We made a guess that the front door must be on the inland side. The last we saw of the lady, she'd shot up and was banging ever so frightenedly on the window behind her, calling, 'Oh, mind, oh, mind!' 'If you ask me,' said Edna, 'this is a loony-bin. But if so, why do they put up "Teas"?'

On the land side of the hotel, the grass went sloping quite steep up. Awful cows had trodden and messed up all over the place. We looked round but we didn't see any cows. There was the hall door, all right, under a glass porch with one pane gone. The door was ever so shut and the bell out of its socket so nothing would do Edna but to start hammering, I'd have ten times sooner gone missing my tea; I could have slapped Edna, being stubborn like that.

'Oh give over, do, Edna,' I was starting to say – when quite of a sudden the door opened and a young fellow looked out – in his shirt-sleeves, he was. He'd come ever so quiet, in those rubber-soled shoes. He didn't smile or frown, he just looked at us – the way he had no expression was quite rude. He held the door half-shut, keeping his hand on it.

'We want tea for two,' said Edna – right out flat.

'Sorry,' he said, 'we don't serve teas.' He stepped back and started shutting the door. But Edna pushed in her shoulder as quick as quick. She started to say, 'Well, what I want to know is——' and I started to ask her to come off it. Then, though, something made me look round at the hill, and – oh, my goodness, I could have dropped! There were those awful cows, the pack of them, awful black cows, with their horns and every-thing, coming downhill behind us ever so stealthy ready to spring on us. I grabbed Edna, and she saw – before we half knew what had happened, we'd fought past the young man in at the door. Edna snatched the door from him and gave it a slam shut. I felt her shake all over, just like a piece of paper. She said, 'My girl friend doesn't like cows.'

The first minute, it was so dark we couldn't see any-thing, it was so dark in there. The place smelled ever so musty. There must have been an archway through to the front; there were chinks of light round the shutters on the sea side. When I started to see, I saw what looked like a row of corpses, all hanging along on the one wall. Later, I noticed these were gentlemen's mackintoshes. I should have told that first go off, by the smell. There they all hung, not moving – why should they move?

Edna said, 'Those cows of yours are not safe.'

He said, 'Those aren't my cows. Are you two from town?'

I daresay Edna gave him one of her looks. She shrilled

up and said, 'Then what about that board?' 'Which board? – Oh, that,' he said, as easy as anything. He walked off like a cat, in his rubber shoes, and began unbolting the shutter we'd seen the light come through. So we saw the sea out through the window, and felt better – a bit. And we saw through there, through the arch, now he'd got the shutter open, a lounge – but no palms, and dust over the mirrors, and wicker chairs and tables all coming untwined. 'We did serve teas, all right,' he said, 'but it isn't convenient now.' He went on, 'Then you two came round by the sea?'

I don't think he meant to cheek us, it was just his manner, I don't think he more than half knew we were there. After a bit he said, 'It seems a shame, doesn't it? Did you come far?' I told him where we'd come from. Then he said, 'Have you two got friends, where you are?'

'What's that to you?' said Edna.

He simply went on, 'If you've got friends, or anyone that you talk to, where you're staying – well, just *don't* talk this time – see? I don't serve teas any more, and I don't serve anything, and I don't want locals or visitors coming nosing round here after teas or anything else that I don't serve.' He stood with his arms crossed and his thumbs tucked under his elbows, looking at Edna and me in the calmest way. 'You've no right in here,' he said. 'This place isn't even open. You wouldn't come pushing in if you were a nice pair of girls. All the same, though' (he said to us like an emperor), 'I'll give you your teas, all right, *if you won't go off and talk.*'

So then I piped up (I could see no harm in it, really) and said, how Edna and I always kept ourselves to ourselves. And I told him we'd be back in London the day after tomorrow. Edna said she wasn't sure that she did fancy her tea now, after one thing and another and what had been said. 'Oh yes, you do,' he said. 'Women always fancy their teas.' He rubbed one hand on a table and rubbed some dust off, then stood and watched the dust on his hand. Then he did something queerer – he went and opened the window and stuck his head right out and looked up and down. Whatever he thought he'd see, it didn't seem to be there. So then he pulled his head in and shut the window and said, 'O.K.; I'll go and see what I've got.'

'You mean, tea?' we said.

'Tea,' he said. 'If you'll sit in those two chairs.' He pulled two chairs out – they were ever so dusty – and stuck the two of us down in a chair each. 'If you move out of those,' he said, 'you won't get any tea. See? And if a lady should pass, you don't have to talk to her – see? The lady's like you, she keeps herself to herself.'

That was the way he went on – as if we'd been a pair of kids. I and Edna dared hardly look at each other – but she put her finger up and gave her forehead a tap. Still, whatever were we to do, just two girls like her and me – and with those cows waiting just outside the door? He got as far as the archway, to give a last look at us. Then he frowned – and we all three looked at the window. There *she* was, the one in blue, with her eyes starting out of her head. She saw him, and began to bang on the glass. I and Edna were sitting back, and so she couldn't see us. We could see her talking away, but we couldn't hear what she said. In the glare out there her blue dress looked ever so queer. She kept banging harder and harder, with the flat of her hands. 'If you don't watch out,' said Edna, 'she'll smash your window. Not that it's my affair.'

For the minute, he seemed to me to quite lose his head. Then he gave us each such a look – like an awful warning, it was – then made a dart at the window and threw it up. Then we *did* hear her – her voice came out in a wail. 'Oh, Oswald, oh, my darling Oswald!' she said.

Before he could step away from the window she reached in, as quick as quick, and got her arms round his neck. 'Oh, I did watch,' she said, 'I *did*! But they got in. Oh, Oswald, forgive me. Forgive me, Oswald,' she said. 'What's going to happen? They'll take you away. I've failed you!' He wriggled his head, but she held on ever so tight. Her wrists were as thin as wire, with gold bracelets slipping into her cuff.

'That's all right, Miss Tope,' he said. 'Nothing's happened; I'm safe, really I am.'

'But they got in. Where are they?'

'They didn't,' he said. 'They've gone.'

She glared past him in at the window – and I tell you, I and Edna stiffened back in our chairs. 'But what did they see?' she said. 'What did they guess? Suppose they're somewhere? Let me come in and look.'

'Ah,' he said, 'but if you come in, who's going to keep look-out? Go back and keep look-out. You know I depend on you.' That made her let him go and come over puzzled for a minute. She stood there puzzling it out, with her eyes fixed on his face. 'I'm *depending* on you,' he said – he was like a father to her. And she could have been his mother – as years go. She looked ready to cry. 'Are you really safe?' she said.

'I'm always safe,' he said, 'while you keep watch.' He gave her a sort of nod, and she crinkled her whole face up and gave him the same sort of nod – then she went away. He waited another minute, then shut the window and walked off, as calm as anything, through the arch.

Well, Edna and I just sat; we stayed in those two chairs and didn't utter or even look at each other. I don't know how that time ever went by. We heard Oswald off somewhere, putting out china, and we could smell the oil stove – he must have left the door open; *he* was listening, all right. Then when he came back and put the tray down he said, 'Well, here you are.' Edna reached for the pot, but he'd got to it first; he pulled up a chair and sat down, ever so at his ease. That was his way of showing we weren't to pay: it was not our tea, it was his. Edna hates being put under compliment – how she did flush up. And I'm sure I was glad to keep my face in my cup. He cut me and Edna each a slice off the loaf. I saw Edna ready to fire up.

'It's all very fine to say not to talk,' she said. 'But how are my friend and me to know what not to talk about? That Miss Tope, I daresay? Whatever is eating her?'

He said, 'She thinks I did a murder.'

'Does she?' said Edna. 'Did you?'

'No,' says he, as offhand as anything. 'But she thinks every minute they'll be coming for me. The fact is, I don't want them coming round after *her*. Her people are all on to get her shut up. They wouldn't care what she suffered. She gave them the slip once, though, and now they don't know she's here. If they did, they'd be round here for her in a jiffy – they don't care *what* she might suffer, wouldn't care if it killed her. But I'd see them all to blazes before I'd let them touch her. I'm the one friend she's got.'

'I must say,' said Edna, 'you take a lot on yourself. Why, she's bats, she is really. She might do anyone harm. Look at those hands of hers – they're as strong as strong.'

'She won't do me harm,' said Oswald.

'She might do herself harm, too.'

'Not while she's with me.'

'Where did she get that, then, about that murder you did?'

Oswald went all quite different when he talked of Miss Tope; he wasn't cool and please-yourself any longer. You might think he was a mother just had her first. 'I kidded her that,' he said. 'If they weren't to come and take her she and I were bound to keep lying low. And when she first came back here she was out all over the place – along the main road, round the village – just like a child, so trustful, talking away to everyone. Of course she got remarked on – how could she not be? Her people would have been here for her in a week. So I had to think up some way to keep her quiet without letting on it was *her*: she'd have died of that. So I told her I'd done something awful, and that they'd be coming for me, and that she'd have to hide me, and keep watch. Since then, she's never budged from this place.'

'Poor soul,' I said.

He said, 'You don't know her. She's as sweet and lovely as she was when a girl.'

'No doubt,' said Edna, 'she is the perfect lady. All the same, she's willing to stay where she thinks there's been a murder done. Do you mean to say *that* didn't give her a turn against you?'

'Why, no,' Oswald said. 'She'd never judge what *I* did. She just sometimes cries and calls me her poor thing. She and I have been like that – friends with each other – since I was a little kid and she was the loveliest girl.

You see her and my fathers, they were so thick – though her father was a rich gentleman; at one time he could have bought England; he had a yacht and all. It was her father set my father up in this business, this hotel. Then they were always coming here, Miss Meena and him. And where Major Tope came, in those days, his crowd used to follow him. Ever so many gentlemen, and Miss Meena – they used to call this their headquarters – my father's place. I remember all these windows blazing down on the sand, and Miss Meena in her lace dress on that veranda, singing to her guitar. She was like a queen to them all – and she was my queen all right. They used to laugh at me, always round after her. But in those days I was only a little kid. When Major Tope's crash came, all that crowd that used to come here melted away like snow. I guess they lost money, too. Major Tope had invested for *my* father all my father had made out of this place. So when the crash came, my father went down too. Major Tope couldn't stand it all; he put himself out. My father wasn't left long after that lot went: I was left with this place, and I did carry on for a bit, just with teas and that, but when Miss Tope came back I shut down. It wouldn't do – not with her.'

'Then you didn't ought to have left that board up, with "Teas"!'

'That's for her,' he said. 'I did try taking it down, once, but how she did take on – she won't see a thing changed. The day she came back she said, "Here I am, back, Oswald. Now we'll be happy. We've always been happy here." She hates to see anything go – I couldn't hurt like that.'

'That's all very well,' said Edna, 'but how ever do you make out? With no custom or anything? You've got your own life to think of – a young fellow like you.'

He said, as stand-offish as anything, 'Oh, I make out all right. This premises is still mine, and I get a bit for the grass.'

'Still, you can't keep on,' Edna said. He said: 'Leave that to her and me.'

He got up and piled back the things on the tray. 'Well, if you must go . . .' he said. 'Thanks for your company.' So she and I got up. When he saw Edna eyeing out of the window he said, 'No, not that way; you're going back inland.' He got us out through the hall – oh, it echoed, it did sound empty – past the mackintoshes all those people had left. 'Well, I'm sure you've been very kind,' I said, 'giving us tea and everything. Thank you, I'm sure.'

'The way to thank me,' he said, 'is by keeping your mouths shut.'

While he was opening the door I said, 'Oh, Edna, the cows!' He gave a sort of grin and said he'd make that all right. As a matter of fact, the cows were off up another hill. Oswald started us off up a path that he said would bring us down again on the sands in the next bay. (And it did.) He stayed, with a stick, as he'd promised, between us and that other hill where the cows were. We walked fast and were ever so out of breath. I looked back once and saw Oswald, looking quite little, and his hotel down there looking just like a little box. I thought when we got our breaths we were bound to start saying something. Then I saw Edna'd put on one of her funny manners, so I didn't say anything – I didn't want to, either. Because what can you say when you don't know what you think? And what can you think when a thing doesn't make sense?

NO. 16

To approach Medusa Terrace by its east corner, on a first visit to the Maximilian Bewdons, was to fancy oneself, for an unnerving minute, the victim of a hoax. Maximilian's only visitors, nowadays, were of the type least able to bear this — idealistic, friendless, new from the provinces: accordingly, unaware of the slump in him. One can make for oneself a pretty picture of the distinguished writer's St. John's Wood home — jasmine outside, *objets d'art* within. Maximilian had not, in fact, been distinguished for fifteen years. But the last circle from the splash he had once made faded slowly — and meanwhile he was able to make a living. The masks on Medusa Terrace had lost their features; the pilasters crumbled; front doors were boarded up.

The differing fortunes of St. John's Wood house property give that uphill landscape a dreamlike inconsistency. To walk there is to have a crazy architectural film, with no music, reeled past. Every corner brings you to something out of the scheme — even without a touch of fever on you (and Jane Oates had more than a touch of fever) some starts of taste or fancy look like catastrophes. Pale tan brick blocks of flats, compressed cities, soar up over studios all trellis and vine. There are gashes and pitted gardens where villas have been torn down. Criss-cross go roads of dun silent stucco, frosted glass porches, grills. A perspective gallops downhill all jade-and-whiteness and bird-song – but you may turn off into a by-street as mean, faded and airless as any in Pimlico. Dotted among the bosky gothic love-nests are vita-glassed mansions, avid for sun and money, still on the agent's lists. Here, a once bewitching villa, now scabrous, awaits the knacker for some obscure shame – next door, its twin is all paintpots and whistling workmen, being dolled up again. The straight roads string all this on an old plan. The stranger feels abnormally keyed up; he finds himself in a sort of nightmare of whim.

Jane Oates's troubled sensations *were* heightened by fever: she had a temperature, had only got up this morning and should have been still in bed. But today – now – she was to meet Maximilian Bewdon for the first time: she would not have failed if she'd had to come from the tomb. Not only influenza but hero worship made her pulses race. His letter, with the invitation to lunch, had been brought to her the first day she was ill, and her thought then had been: I must go if I die. So images had swum through her drowsy days and made her delirious nights ecstatic. Here she was, on her way to Medusa Terrace – too eager, she had got off the bus too soon. Her feet were lead, her spine ached, her head sang, glassily clear.

The thaw had left London glistening, supine, sunny. From gardens the snow, swept up into mounds, had not gone yet. Jane had come on buses from Battersea Park; she was not a Londoner; she had not been up here before. Everything, in this maze of trees and doorways as she walked towards Maximilian, gave her its message or mystery. The sun still hurt her still rather weak eyes.

She had the stolid, untroubled beauty of a mature country girl, and a touch of old-fashioned style.

In the autumn, about three months ago, Jane's book had been published. It was a naive book, but sufficiently disconcerting, and *new* – too new to go far unless it should happen to catch some important eye. She had no friends (in London), no one to make a splash. So the publisher gave the book an agreeable format, a vermilion cover with a chalky surface, gave one or two luncheons for Jane (at which she could not speak) and hoped for a *succès d'estime*. Maximilian, reviewing for an obscure paper, had not only 'done' the book but had made a feature of it. The publisher shrugged when he got the cutting and saw Maximilian's name. But Jane's cup was full. She got the column by heart and, for days, sang a Magnificat. That *he* should have written this – and that he should have written *this*. Her liberation into this sudden book could have been all: but now she was truly crowned. She wrote Maximilian a humble letter, confessing the hero worship of years. Since she was seventeen (she was now thirty) she had hardly missed a word Maximilian signed. She was deeply feeling; she lived alone in the country. She was a true enough artist to have false taste – for the ignorant artist, like the savage, is attracted by what is glittering: by the time he learns what is what, some virtue is gone already.

Maximilian Bewdon, after about a week, had replied to Jane's letter: they started to correspond. Though her book was prose she wrote poems also, she told him, but she was shy of those. She learned that he was married; he asked her if she were married; she answered that she had never been in love. Before Christmas, she was able to write and tell him she was coming to London, to share a flat for three months with a friend who lived in Battersea Park. When she got to Battersea Park, already ill, she got his letter, bidding her bring the poems to lunch.

So here they were, in a folder under her arm. She was not nervous; fever floated her or distilled her out of herself. But when she turned the corner into Medusa Terrace, Jane Oates stopped – like everyone else. She instinctively put her hand up, then took her hand from her eyes to see the same thing again – that north-facing terrace of cracked stucco, dank in its own shadow, semi-ruinous, hollow, full of sealed-up echoes. Doors nailed up, windows boarded or stony with grime. In the gardens, the snow was trodden black. The place so much expected an instant doom, one felt unsafe standing near it.

'*Am* I——? Or, *could* he have——?'

Jane looked up at the numbers stuck on the broken fanlights. Still at the 1's and 2's – he had said, No. 16. Plunging into the shadow with a shiver – she had kept to the sunny sides of the streets – she walked the length of the façade. At the end she dared look up: the last house *was* No. 16. Through less dusty panes she saw curtains like orange ghosts. A shaft of sun struck through from a back window, through a bunch of balloons hung in an arch. This one end house was tacked, living, to the hulk of the terrace. She turned up the steps and rang.

When she had rung twice, a lady came to the door, knocking back a strand of grey hair from her eyes. She eyed Jane and eyed the folder of poems. 'Oh dear – I hope you are not Miss Oates?'

'I——'

'Oh dear. I had wired to put you off: you did not seem

to be on the telephone. My husband has been ill for several days; he's just up, but not fit to see anyone. He only remembered this morning that you were coming, or I should have – I *am* sorry. Oh dear.'

At these words Jane, in her feverish weakness, sweated: she saw sweat and a flush break out on the lady's forehead, and Mrs. Bewdon put up a hand and said: 'We've had influenza.' 'I've had it too.' 'It seems to be everywhere.' 'I'm sorry I didn't get your telegram: I started early, it was a long way——'

'Nancy,' said a voice from inside a room, 'let Miss Oates come in.'

So Jane, unable to say anything further, was let into the shabby, decent hall – an oak chest with letters stamped for posting, prints hung on the paper seamed with damp, a humid smell of broth. She turned through a door to face Maximilian, who stood in the archway, underneath the bunch of coloured balloons. She heard the roar of two antique gasfires, one in the dark front room, one in the sunny back, and saw Maximilian's figure crucified on the sunshine in an extravagance of apology. 'What must you think?' he said. She stood blind, the sun in her eyes, and could not think anything. There was a moment's silence, while Jane shifted the folder, pressing it with the thumb of her woollen glove. Then he said: 'Thank you for missing the telegram.'

'But I must go.'

'No, you mustn't go. There *is* lunch.' He reached out – the act seemed vague and belated like an act in a dream – and shook Jane's hot, dry hand in his hotter and drier hand. 'Now you're here,' he said.

'But you're ill.'

'Still, I'm here,' he said, with an obstinate frown.

They sat down beside each other on the sofa, and she saw his exposed-looking forehead, the spectacles through which he sent, obliquely, a look at once baited and fiery, the short hands wasting their force in uneasy, fleeting, nervous touches on things. Maximilian looked about fifty; he looked frustrated and spent. His hair, weak as fur, flowed back and he wore a little moustache. He said, with an accusing smile: 'You thought I had gone.'

'Yes, I did, when I first came to the Terrace.'

'That's what they all think – that lets them out, don't you see. They take one look and go home. "He'd gone," they say to the others. Lots don't start at all. "We don't know where he is now. They've pulled down where he once was. There's no tracing him——" '

'How *can* you?' Jane said gently. Maximilian repeated: 'It lets them out. That's my tact.'

Jane, looking apprehensively round at the room, said: 'But some day, I suppose, it *will* happen?'

'Oh, we'll be pulled down all right,' said Maximilian, pressing his forehead.

'If the idea upsets you——'

Mrs. Bewdon, laying the front room table, said: 'The idea does not upset my husband at all. When we move, he will miss it. We are let keep this house on from week to week: when the men come, they'll begin at the other end. They work fast, I daresay, and it will be so noisy. So *then* we shall have to think——'

'I am so sorry,' said Jane.

'I shan't be sorry,' said Mrs. Bewdon. 'That will be something settled.' She bent to straighten a fork. 'But he – I – we cannot bear to decide. . . .'

Her husband said: 'One decides quickly enough when there is any question of desire.'

'It's so long since the last of our neighbours left: they expected something to happen, but nothing has, as you see. At the same time, it's still a shock to find *nobody* else. It is not as though this house stood by itself. When we cannot sleep, or when we are at all ill . . . For instance, since my husband has been ill he keeps hearing the piano next door. "Go in," he said to me yesterday, "and tell her how much I like her playing. Ask her to go on playing———" Yes, you *did*, Maximilian, but No. 15 is empty; it's nailed up; there is a crack under the balcony.'

She looked through the arch at her husband, laughing not altogether kindly.

'The house suits me,' he said. 'Are we going to have no lunch?' Mrs. Bewdon picked up her tray and floundered out of the room.

A slight steam came from the dishes. Jane Oates could taste nothing: she scalded her mouth with the broth, and the fish pie lay on her tongue like wadding. The Bewdons put up an even less good show. She no longer heard what was said, or heard if anything *was* said: before the end of lunch she had to stop and rest her brow on her hands. Maximilian poured himself out a glass of water. The sun wheeled off the face of the extinct terrace opposite: reflections no longer entered the north room. Someone left the table, and when Jane raised her forehead Maximilian said, 'Nancy has gone to make the coffee.'

'Oh, it will be too hot.'

Maximilian agreed: 'This is the worst time of day.'

She looked: behind his and her figures she saw bookshelves, in the flat, fading light. She looked up, at the cracks across the ceiling and at the bunch of balloons – air must have escaped from them, for they were already flaccid like old grapes. 'Why are those balloons there?'

'A man peddled them up and down the terrace, so I had to buy them all.'

'That was kind.'

'He held me responsible.' Maximilian hitched one elbow over the back of his chair; he turned away from Jane with a quick, rather frenzied movement.

'Mr. Bewdon, I ought not to make you talk.'

'We shan't meet again like this – for the first time. We shan't meet again when we don't know what we are saying.'

Birds and waterfalls sounded in Jane's head, so that when Mrs. Bewdon brought in the tray of coffee and poured out, talking, Jane sat not listening but smiling. 'Maximilian, you're not drinking your coffee. It's no use to sit twisting round from the light. Miss Oates will excuse you: you must go and lie down.'

'Miss Oates must stay with me, to read her poems.'

'Well you may read, Miss Oates, but he must not say anything. When he goes to sleep, creep away, if you don't mind. I'm going up to lie down in my own room. It will do me good.'

Maximilian went through the arch and lay down on the sofa in the back room: Mrs. Bewdon tucked a rug over his feet, and soon the gas fire drew a scorched smell from the rug. For some time one heard Mrs. Bewdon walking about upstairs; then a spring cracked in her bed as *she* lay down. Maximilian crossed his hands over his eyes; Jane undid the folder of poems and sat on a low chair, one elbow on the typewriting table so that she could prop her cheek on her hand. The wintry sun no longer afflicted them; it sent rays obliquely across the garden, through the boughs of a tree. Jane did not know she knew her poems by heart, but now she heard herself speak them as though she had been hypnotized. It frightened her not to know what was coming next – and she felt something mounting up round her in the dusk, was again frightened, did not know where it came from. Whenever she stopped, the outdoor silence pressed as close as suspense: you had the sensation of a great instrument out there in London, unstruck.

Jane kept her eyes down as though she were reading, but when she paused she looked towards Maximilian – at his face pitched up unkindly by the end of the sofa, and at his eye-bandage of knotted hands. All at once he said: 'Stop.'

She broke off a line.

'You're so beautiful.'

'But your hands are over your eyes.'

'I remember you coming in and standing there in the sun. So ill, when I am so ill. You might be a lovely neighbour. You played the piano yesterday.'

'I was ill yesterday.'

'Then you did play the piano – Come over here, Jane.'

Jane dropped the poems and knelt by the sofa. Maximilian uncovered his eyes – after a moment he caught at her two wrists and held them so that her fingers were pressed to his temples. 'Fever and pain,' he said. 'You make me hear the piano. What do you hear?'

'A waterfall in my head.' She felt her pulse jumping inside his grip and said: 'We are making each other iller.' He had shut his eyes; she looked at his face and said: 'I wish I had cool hands.'

'If you had cool hands you would go away. I shall lose you when you are well.' Pressing her fingers close to his temples he said: 'All this will be gone – where we are – not a rack left. There'll be no "here" left – how can you come back?' Then he let go her wrists roughly. 'But I don't want you to come again.'

'Why?'

'You'd soon see why.'

'But my poems. . . .'

'Take them away. Burn them. You'll only lose your way.'

'Are you lost?'

'Yes, I'm lost. You don't understand yet. We only know when we're ill – the piano inside my head, the waterfall inside yours. My image of you, that neighbourly image. Eternity is inside us – it's a secret that we must never, never, never try to betray. Look where just *time* has brought me; look at where it's left me. When you make friends, don't talk about me.'

'You praised my book,' she said wildly starting up.

'I've got to live. How could I write, in a paper, "She should have burned her hands off before she wrote"?'

'Are we not to believe in each other?'

'Come back here; put your head beside me.' Maximilian rolled his head sideways on the end of the sofa, and, sitting back on her heels on the ground beside him, Jane laid her head where he had made room. Maximilian's voice went drowsy; his eyes closed. 'You sweet neighbour,' he said. 'You sweet, distempered friend.'

'But Shakespeare . . .'

'Go to sleep, Jane, never mind, go to sleep.'

Mrs. Bewdon woke and came down to make tea. She fumbled her way to the kitchen, where she put on the kettle, then into the back room, where she turned the light on and saw Jane and Bewdon asleep with their foreheads together: he lying, she kneeling twisted beside the sofa. They looked like a suicide pact. The room smelled of the scorching of Bewdon's rug. Mrs. Bewdon, when she had drawn the curtains, stooped and gave Jane's shoulder a light pat. 'Tea-time,' she said.

Jane opened her eyes, and Mrs. Bewdon gave her a hand up. Maximilian went on breathing stertorously.

'I ought to go.'

'Oh, I should have something hot first. You don't look really fit to be out at all. He'll sleep on,' she said, without a glance at the sofa, 'so you can slip away just when you like.'

The two women, at tea in the front room, talked low, so as not to wake Maximilian. They did not want to wake him for their peace sake. Jane learned, from the way Mrs. Bewdon spoke of her husband, that she felt a dogged, loyal, unsmiling, unloving pity for him. Mrs. Bewdon's demoralized manner seemed to come from her opinion that she did not live with a real man. She must have married during some delusion of youth.

Mrs. Bewdon's kindness to Jane was profoundly chagrining. Mrs. Bewdon said: 'It's been kind of you to have come. Such a long way – I hope it has been worth while. I'm sorry my husband was not more himself, but you know what influenza is. He's always interested in young writers, though I'm afraid he's inclined to discourage them. He likes to say to them "Don't write".'

'Do they mind?'

'They think it is just his fun,' said Mrs. Bewdon, looking round for the sugar. 'Or else they think he is jealous. But he does really take an interest in them. He's disappointed they don't come back.'

Jane tried to feel sorry for the sleeping man. She still felt herself closely bound to him – he had done no more than hold her wrists, but she was a girl who had never been touched. Now, the indifference in Mrs. Bewdon's voice, and her half-understanding, brought everything low. He has lost me, too, she thought. I shall be unhappy when I am well again.

'Oh, must you be going?' said Mrs. Bewdon. 'Perhaps you are right, though: your eyes look rather ill. Shall I ring up a taxi?'

'No thank you; I can't afford one.'

'Don't forget your poems,' said Mrs. Bewdon, running back for the folder, 'I expect they are good.' Jane heard Bewdon, the other side of the archway, turn over and exclaim something in his sleep – one of those sleeping protests. Running quickly away from his helplessness, she followed Mrs. Bewdon into the hall. The hall door, opened by Mrs. Bewdon, showed cracked steps dropping into the dark. 'You must walk past some day,' said Mrs. Bewdon, 'and see if we are still here.'

The terrace gave out a hundred hollow echoes and, as the door shut, just perceptibly shook. The lamplight picked out its sad face. Not a step but Jane's on the pavement; not a note from the piano. They stared at Jane when she got into the bus . . . On the Battersea Park hall table she found the telegram: she pushed away her poems behind her bureau but took the telegram to her cold bed. Through the night, she kept starting up,

switching her lamp on: she re-read *Should not see anyone.*
In the dark again she heard Bewdon's voice saying
'Sleep . . .' Her pillow sounded hollow with notes and
knockings, notes and knockings you hear in condemned
rooms.

A QUEER HEART

MRS. CADMAN got out of the bus backwards. No amount of practice ever made her more agile; the trouble she had with her big bulk amused everyone, and herself. Gripping the handles each side of the bus door so tightly that the seams of her gloves cracked, she lowered herself cautiously, like a climber, while her feet, overlapping her smart shoes, uneasily scrabbled at each step. One or two people asked why the bus made, for one passenger, such a long, dead stop. But on the whole she was famous on this line, for she was constantly in and out of town. The conductor waited behind her, smiling, holding her basket, arms wide to catch her if she should slip.

Having got safe to the ground, Mrs. Cadman shook herself like a satisfied bird. She took back her shopping-basket from the conductor and gave him a smile instead. The big, kind, scarlet bus once more ground into movement, off up the main road hill; it made a fading blur in the premature autumn dusk. Mrs. Cadman almost waved after it, for with it went the happy part of her day. She turned down the side road that led to her gate.

A wet wind of autumn, smelling of sodden gardens, blew in her face and tilted her hat. Leaves whirled along it, and one lime leaf, as though imploring shelter, lodged in her fur collar. Every gust did more to sadden the poor trees. This was one of those roads outside growing provincial cities that still keep their rural mystery. They seem to lead into something still not known. Traffic roars past one end, but the other end is in silence: you see a wood, a spire, a haughty manor gate, or your view ends with the turn of an old wall. Here some new, raw-looking villas stood with spaces between them; in the spaces were orchards and market-gardens. A glasshouse roof reflected the wet grey light; there was a shut chapel farther along. And, each standing back in half an acre of ground, there were two or three stucco houses with dark windows, sombre but at the same time ornate, built years ago in this then retired spot. Dead lime leaves showered over their grass plots and evergreens. Mrs. Cadman's house, Granville, was one of these: its name was engraved in scrolls over the porch. The solid house was not large, and Mrs. Cadman's daughter, Lucille, could look after it with a daily help.

The widow and her daughter lived here in the state of cheerless meekness Lucille considered suitable for them now. *Mr.* Cadman had liked to have everything done in style. But twelve years ago he had died, travelling on business, in an hotel up in the North. Always the gentleman, he had been glad to spare them this upset at home. He had been brought back to the Midlands for his impressive funeral, whose size showed him a popular man. How unlike Mr. Cadman was Rosa proving herself. One can be most unfriendly in one's way of dying. Ah, well, one chooses one's husband; one's sister is dealt out to one by fate.

Mrs. Cadman, thumb on the latch of her own gate, looked for a minute longer up and down the road –

deeply, deeply unwilling to go in. She looked back at the corner where the bus had vanished, and an immense sigh heaved up her coat lapels and made a cotton carnation, pinned to the fur, brush a fold of her chin. Laced, hooked, buttoned so tightly into her clothes, she seemed to need to deflate herself by these sudden sighs, by yawns or by those explosions of laughter that often vexed Lucille. Through her face – embedded in fat but still very lively, as exposed, as ingenuous as a little girl's – you could see some emotional fermentation always at work in her. Her smiles were frequent, hopeful and quick. Her pitching walk was due to her tight shoes.

When she did go in she went in with a sort of rush. She let the door bang back on the hall wall, so that the chain rattled and an outraged clatter came from the letter-box. Immediately, she knew she had done wrong. Lucille, appalled, looked out of the dining-room. '*Shissssssh!* How can you, mother?' she said.

'Ever so sorry, dear,' said Mrs. Cadman, cast down.

'She'd just dropped off,' said Lucille. 'After her bad night and everything. It really does seem hard.'

Mrs. Cadman quite saw that it did. She glanced nervously up the stairs, then edged into the dining-room. It was not cheerful in here: a monkey puzzle, too close to the window, drank the last of the light up; the room still smelt of dinner; the fire smouldered resentfully, starved for coal. The big mahogany furniture lowered, with no shine. Mrs. Cadman, putting her basket down on the table, sent an uncertain smile across at Lucille, whose glasses blankly gleamed high up on her long face. She often asked herself where Lucille could have come from. *Could* this be the baby daughter she had borne, and tied pink bows on, and christened a pretty name? In the sun in this very bow window she had gurgled into sweet-smelling creases of Lucille's neck — one summer lost in time.

'You *have* been an age,' Lucille said.

'Well, the shops were quite busy. I never *saw*,' she said with irrepressible pleasure, 'I never *saw* so many people in town!'

Lucille, lips tighter than ever shut, was routing about, unpacking the shopping basket, handling the packages. Chemist's and grocer's parcels. Mrs. Cadman watched her with apprehension. Then Lucille pounced; she held up a small, soft parcel in frivolous wrappings. 'Oho,' she said. 'So you've been in at Babbington's?'

'Well, I missed one bus, so I had to wait for the next. So I just popped in there a minute out of the cold. And, you see, I've been wanting a little scarf——'

'Little scarf!' said Lucille. 'I don't know what to make of you, mother. I don't really. How *could* you, at such a time? How you ever could have the heart!' Lucille, standing the other side of the table, leaned across it, her thin weight on her knuckles. This brought her face near her mother's. 'Can't you understand?' she said. 'Can't you take *anything* in? The next little scarf *you'll* need to buy will be black!'

'What a thing to say!' exclaimed Mrs. Cadman, profoundly offended. 'With that poor thing upstairs now, waiting to have her tea.'

'Tea? She can't take her tea. Why, since this morning she can't keep a thing down.'

Mrs. Cadman blenched and began unbuttoning her coat. Lucille seemed to feel that her own prestige and Aunt Rosa's entirely hung on Aunt Rosa's approaching death. You could feel that she and her aunt had thought up this plan together. These last days had been the climax of their complicity. And there was Mrs. Cadman – as ever, as usual – put in the wrong, frowned upon, out of things. Whenever Rosa arrived to stay Mrs. Cadman had no fun in her home, and now Rosa was leaving for ever it seemed worse. A perverse kick of the heart, a flicker of naughtiness, made Mrs. Cadman say: 'Oh, well, while there's life there's hope.'

Lucille said: 'If you won't face it, you won't. But I just say it does fall heavy on me . . . We had the vicar round here this afternoon. He was up with Aunt for a bit, then he looked in and said he did feel I needed a prayer too. He said he thought I was wonderful. He asked where you were, and he seemed to wonder you find the heart to stay out so long. I thought from his manner he wondered a good deal.'

Mrs. Cadman, with an irrepressible titter, said: 'Give him something to think about! Why if I'd ha' shown up that vicar'd have popped out as fast as he popped in. Thinks I'd make a mouthful of him. Why, I've made him bolt down the street. Well, well. He's not *my* idea of a vicar. When your father and I first came here we had a rural dean. Oh, he was as pleasant as anything.'

Lucille, with the air of praying for Christian patience, folded her lips. Jabbing her fingers down the inside of her waistbelt, she more tightly tucked in her tight blouse. She liked looking like Mrs. Noah – no, *Miss* Noah. 'The doctor's not been again. We're to let him know of any change.'

'Well, let's do the best we can,' said Mrs. Cadman. 'But don't keep on *talking*. You don't make things any better, keeping on going on. My opinion is one should keep bright to the last. When my time comes, oh, I would like a cheery face.'

'It's well for you . . .' began Lucille. She bit the remark off and, gathering up the parcels, stalked scornfully out of the dining-room. Without comment she left exposed on the table a small carton of goodies Mrs. Cadman had bought to cheer herself up with and had concealed in the toe of the shopping bag. Soon, from the kitchen came the carefully muffled noises of Lucille putting away provisions and tearing the wrappings off the chemist's things. Mrs. Cadman, reaching out for the carton, put a peppermint into each cheek. She, oh so badly, wanted a cup of tea but dared not follow Lucille into the kitchen in order to put the kettle on.

Though, after all, Granville *was* her house. . . .

You would not think it was her house – not when Rosa was there. While Lucille and her mother were *tête à tête* Lucille's disapproval was at least fairly tacit. But as soon as Rosa arrived on one of these yearly autumn visits – always choosing the season when Mrs. Cadman felt in her least good form, the fall of the leaf – the aunt and niece got together and found everything wrong. Their two cold natures ran together. They found Mrs. Cadman lacking; they forbade the affection she would have offered them. They censured her the whole time. Mrs. Cadman could date her real alienation from Lucille from the year when Rosa's visits began. During Mr. Cadman's lifetime Rosa had never come for more than an afternoon. Mr. Cadman had been his wife's defence from her sister – a great red kind of rumbustious fortification. He had been a man who kept every chill wind out. Rosa, during those stilted afternoon visits, had adequately succeeded in conveying that she found marriage *low*. She might just have suffered a pious marriage; she openly deprecated this high living, this state of fleshly bliss. In order not to witness it too closely she lived on in lodgings in her native town . . . But once widowhood left her sister exposed, Rosa started flapping round Granville like a doomful bird. She instituted these yearly visits, which, she made plain at the same time, gave her not much pleasure. The journey was tedious, and by breaking her habits, leaving her lodgings, Rosa was, out of duty, putting herself about. Her joyless and intimidating visits had, therefore, only one object – to protect the interests of Lucille.

Mrs. Cadman had suspected for some time that Rosa had something the matter with her. No one looks as yellow as that for nothing. But she was not sufficiently intimate with her sister to get down to the cosy subject of insides. This time, Rosa arrived looking worse than ever, and three days afterwards had collapsed. Lucille said now she had known her aunt was poorly. Lucille said now she had always known. 'But of course you wouldn't notice, mother,' she said.

Mrs. Cadman sat down by the fire and, gratefully, kicked off her tight shoes. In the warmth her plump feet uncurled, relaxed, expanded like sea-anemones. She stretched her legs out, propped her heels on the fender and wiggled her toes voluptuously. They went on wiggling of their own accord: they seemed to have an independent existence. Here, in her home, where she felt so 'put wrong' and chilly, they were like ten stout, confidential friends. She said, out loud: 'Well, *I* don't know what I've done.'

The fact was: Lucille and Rosa resented her. (She'd feel better when she had had her tea.) She should *not*

have talked as she had about the vicar. But it seemed
so silly, Lucille having just him. She did wish Lucille
had a better time. No young man so much as paused at
the gate. Lucille's aunt had wrapped her own dank
virginity round her like someone sharing a mackintosh.

Mrs. Cadman had had a good time. A real good time
always lasts: you have it with all your nature and all
your nature stays living with it. She had been a pretty
child with long, blonde hair that her sister Rosa, who
was her elder sister, used to tweak when they were alone
in their room. She had grown used, in that childish
attic bedroom, to Rosa's malevolent silences. Then one
had grown up, full of great uppish curves. Hilda Cadman
could sing. She had sung at parties and sung at charity
concerts, too. She had been invited from town to town,
much fêted in business society. She had sung in a dress
cut low at the bosom, with a rose or carnation tucked into
her hair. She had drunk port wine in great red rooms
blazing with chandeliers. Mr. Cadman had whisked her
away from her other gentlemen friends, and not for a
moment had she regretted it. Nothing had been too
good for her: she had gone on singing. She had felt warm
air on her bare shoulders; she still saw the kind, flushed
faces crowding round. Mr. Cadman and she belonged to
the jolly set. They all thought the world of her, and she
thought the world of them.

Mrs. Cadman, picking up the poker, jabbed the fire
into a spurt of light. It does not do any good to sit and
think in the dark.

The town was not the same now. They had all died,
or lost their money, or gone. But you kept on loving the
town for its dear old sake. She sometimes thought:
Why not move and live at the seaside, where there would

be a promenade and a band? But she knew her nature clung to the old scenes; where you had lived, you lived – your nature clung like a cat. While there was *something* to look at she was not one to repine. It kept you going to keep out and about. Things went, but then new things came in their place. You can't cure yourself of the habit of loving life. So she drank up the new pleasures – the big cafés, the barging buses, the cinemas, the shops dripping with colour, almost all built of glass. She could be perfectly happy all alone in a café, digging into a cream bun with a fork, the band playing, smiling faces all round. The old faces had not gone: they had dissolved, diluted into the ruddy blur through which she saw everything.

Meanwhile, Lucille was hard put to it, living her mother down. Mother looked ridiculous, always round town like that.

Mrs. Cadman heard Lucille come out of the kitchen and go upstairs with something rattling on a tray. She waited a minute more, then sidled into the kitchen, where she cautiously started to make tea. The gas-ring, as though it were a spy of Lucille's, popped loudly when she applied the match.

'Mother, she's asking for you.'

'Oh, dear – do you mean she's——?'

'She's much more herself this evening,' Lucille said implacably.

Mrs. Cadman, at the kitchen table, had been stirring sugar into her third cup. She pushed her chair back, brushed crumbs from her bosom and followed Lucille like a big, unhappy lamb. The light was on in the hall, but the stairs led up into shadow: she had one more start

of reluctance at their foot. Autumn draughts ran about
in the top storey: up there the powers of darkness all
seemed to mobilize. Mrs. Cadman put her hand on the
banister knob. 'Are you sure she *does* want to see me?
Oughtn't she to stay quiet?'

'You should go when she's asking. You never
know. . . .'

Breathless, breathing unevenly on the top landing,
Mrs. Cadman pushed open the spare-room – that was
the sick-room – door. In there – in here – the air was
dead, and at first it seemed very dark. On the ceiling an
oil-stove printed its flower-pattern; a hooded lamp, low
down, was turned away from the bed. On that dark
side of the lamp she could just distinguish Rosa, propped
up, with the sheet drawn to her chin.

'Rosa?'

'Oh, it's you?'

'Yes; it's me, dear. Feeling better this evening?'

'Seemed funny, you not coming near me.'

'They said for you to keep quiet.'

'My own sister . . . You never liked sickness, did you?
Well, I'm going. I shan't trouble you long.'

'Oh, don't talk like that!'

'I'm glad to be going. Keeping on lying here . . . We
all come to it. Oh, give over crying, Hilda. Doesn't do
any good.'

Mrs. Cadman sat down, to steady herself. She
fumbled in her lap with her handkerchief, perpetually,
clumsily knocking her elbows against the arms of the
wicker chair. 'It's such a shame,' she said. 'It's such a
pity. You and me, after all . . .'

'Well, it's late for all that now. Each took our own
ways.' Rosa's voice went up in a sort of ghostly sharpness.

'There were things that couldn't be otherwise. I've tried to do right by Lucille. Lucille's a good girl, Hilda. You should ask yourself if you've done right by her.'

'Oh, for shame, Rosa,' said Mrs. Cadman, turning her face through the dark towards that disembodied voice. 'For shame, Rosa, even if you *are* going. You know best what's come between her and me. It's been you and her, you and her. I don't know where to turn some-times——'

Rosa said: 'You've got such a shallow heart.'

'How should you know? Why, you've kept at a distance from me ever since we were tots. Oh, I know I'm a great silly, always after my fun, but I never took what was yours; I never did harm to you. I don't see what call we have got to judge each other. You didn't want my life that I've had.'

Rosa's chin moved: she was lying looking up at her sister's big rippling shadow, splodged up there by the light of the low lamp. It is frightening, having your shadow watched. Mrs. Cadman said: 'But what did I do to you?'

'I *could* have had a wicked heart,' said Rosa. 'A vain, silly heart like yours. I could have fretted, seeing you take everything. One thing, then another. But I was shown. God taught me to pity you. God taught me my lesson . . . You wouldn't even remember that Christmas tree.'

'What Christmas tree?'

'No, you wouldn't even remember. Oh, I thought it was lovely. I could have cried when they pulled the curtains open, and there it was, all blazing away with candles and silver and everything——'

'Well, isn't that funny? I——'

'No; you've had all that pleasure since. All of us older children couldn't take it in, hardly, for quite a minute or two. It didn't look real. Then I looked up, and there was a fairy doll fixed on the top, right on the top spike, fixed on to a star. I set my heart on her. She had wings and long, fair hair, and she was shining away. I couldn't take my eyes off her. They cut the presents down; but she wasn't for anyone. In my childish blindness I kept praying to God. If I am not to have her, I prayed, let her stay there.'

'And what did God do?' Hilda said eagerly.

'Oh, He taught me and saved me. You were a little thing in a blue sash; you piped up and asked might you have the doll.'

'Fancy me! Aren't children awful!' said Mrs. Cadman. 'Asking like that.'

'They said: "Make her sing for it." They were taken with you. So you piped up again, singing. You got her, all right. I went off where they kept the coats. I've thanked God ever since for what I had to go through! I turned my face from vanity from that very night. I had been shown.'

'Oh, what a shame!' said Hilda. 'Oh, I think it was cruel; you poor little mite.'

'No; I used to see that doll all draggled about the house till no one could bear the sight of it. I said to myself: that's how those things end. Why, I'd learnt more in one evening than you've ever learnt in your life. Oh, yes, I've watched you, Hilda. Yes, and I've pitied you.'

'Well, you showed me no pity.'

'You asked for no pity – all vain and set up.'

'No wonder you've been against me. Fancy me not

knowing. I didn't *mean* any harm – why, I was quite a little thing. I don't even remember.'

'Well, you'll remember one day. When you lie as I'm lying you'll find that everything comes back. And you'll see what it adds up to.'

'Well, if I do?' said Hilda. 'I haven't been such a baby; I've seen things out in my own way; I've had my ups and downs. It hasn't been all jam.' She got herself out of the armchair and came and stood uncertainly by the foot of the bed. She had a great wish to reach out and turn the hooded lamp round, so that its light could fall on her sister's face. She felt she should *see* her sister, perhaps for the first time. Inside the flat, still form did implacable disappointment, then, stay locked? She wished she could give Rosa some little present. Too late to give Rosa anything pretty now: she looked back – it had always, then, been too late? She thought: you poor queer heart; you queer heart, eating yourself out, thanking God for the pain. She thought: I did that to her; then what have I done to Lucille?

She said: 'You're ever so like me, Rosa, really, aren't you? Setting our hearts on things. When you've got them you don't notice. No wonder you wanted Lucille . . . You did ought to have had that fairy doll.'

THE GIRL WITH THE STOOP

A SMALL summer town, seaside, in the late rainy autumn has a left-behind air. Simply to live here is not fully to live – and Tibbie, a summer girl, a born holiday-maker, had not learnt yet how to feel like a resident. Very few things ruffled her calm nature, but she did not feel at ease in her aunt's house. In this villa, everyone except Tibbie seemed to be always going up or down the stairs: Tibbie felt she could seldom fully relax . . . This was a Wednesday morning, about eleven; she had washed three pairs of silk stockings and written a picture postcard, and that seemed to be all she had to do. For some time she watched the rain from the bow window, while desultorily teasing her aunt's cat. Then, though it did not stop raining, the sky lightened a little; brighter reflections appeared on the wet bushes, the wet asphalt garden path. Tibbie feared to linger in the drawing-room – her aunt might come down and find something for her to do. So she heaved herself out of the armchair with a sigh, unhung her mackintosh from the hall rack, buttoned herself to the chin, tucked her curls inside an oil-silk hood, and went out – went out with no object at all.

The residential road led straight down to the sea. Behind their neat, white gates the villas were in a torpor: all the people in them might have died in their sleep.

She did not even wonder whether they had. The fish-monger's boy, in a glistening mackintosh cape, bicycled slowly past her, whistling a little flat. He just gave her a look, but she did not even see him. The wet, salt air met her forehead, creeping under her hood. Her face, with the long nose dustily freckled, the sweet, mild, crumpled, indeterminate mouth, lolled a little forward over her high collar, like a flower without the sense to grow up straight.

Tibbie was staying here with her Aunt Cara simply to put in time. She was engaged to be married; she should be making her trousseau; she had brought lengths of pink ninon to sew. The young man was in India; he had proposed by letter; in April he would return to claim his inert bride. Aunt Cara, in common with the other relations, supposed marriage might pull Tibbie together. She was sorry to see so few letters go to the mail, fearing Tibbie might let the young man slip. She pointed out to Tibbie how many nice English girls were to be met in India, and how neglect tries the most faithful young man's heart. But Tibbie would say: 'Oh, no, Tom loves me, I'm sure.'

This morning, the sea front was void and dejected-looking. The tide was out, leaving stretches of dead sand. The empty bandstand dripped; drops slipped through the slats of seats. Tibbie's equable little heart sank. But one reach of the promenade she always walked down with pleasure – she looked forward to passing the Palace Hotel. This great de luxe hotel, dazzlingly white and lofty, all glass lounges, balconies, boxes of flowers, and with its cascade of marble steps, was the chief glory of the quiet resort. Even in autumn it had a sort of season: rich convalescents stayed there, or people who played golf. At tea time a band played; all day long maroon pages could be seen at attention inside the revolving door. Yes, even to dawdle past the Palace Hotel was to feel oneself lapped by its sumptuous mystery . . . Ungloved hands plunged shyly in her mackintosh pockets, Tibbie, unbending her stoop a little, threw up the look of a dreamer at the sun lounge windows, those great steamy vistas of plate-glass.

Francis, leaning forward against the plate-glass window, gripping the arms of his cripple's chair, cried: 'There she goes! There goes that girl with the stoop!'

'Does she?' said Geoff, unmoved, inside *Esquire.* Then he remembered he ought to humour Francis; he looked politely over the magazine. Indoor hotel life made Geoff apathetic; this morning the too-rich breakfast lay on his stomach; the steam heating put a band round his head.

'She looked at us, too,' said Francis. He added, knitting his forehead: 'I wonder where she's off to?'

'She isn't in any hurry. Where could a girl be off to, in this hole?'

Francis flushed and immediately said, stiffly: 'Oh, all right, all right; I know it's a frightful place. For God's sake get out if you're bored. Why don't you get back to London? I don't want anyone martyred because of me.'

'Oh, shut up. I didn't mean it like that.'

Geoff said to himself that that was the worst of Francis – things kept being so tricky the whole time. You never knew where you might put your foot next. Francis had been sent down here by his rich father for a blow of sea air before the winter set in, and Geoff, his big, ordinary first cousin, was there, too, as a guest, to cheer Francis up. The boys were the same age, but matters of health and money created a rather cruel contrast between them. Geoff, born hard up, had been glad to accept the place in the family business that should have been Francis's. He had been given a week's leave from the business to come down here and live like a fighting cock. But his animal charm and his animal spirits wilted; he failed to cheer Francis up, and he did not have much fun. He longed to go off to golf, but that seemed shabby: not part of the bargain of being here. Altogether, he felt rather a flop. It was Francis who had first called this place a hole, but Geoff saw now he had been wrong to agree . . . On fine days they would go up and down the sea front, Francis adeptly steering his motor chair. This morning it was too wet to do even that. Anxious to make amends, Geoff put down *Esquire* and looked politely after his cousin's girl with the stoop. 'Well, she's not my type,' he said, as nicely as ever. 'But, of course, you can't really judge, in a mackintosh.'

'She blinks like that at us every time we see her. She's so shy and vague – she's exactly perfect, I think.'

'Well, that seems too bad – I don't see what one can do. She's not quite the sort of girl one could——'

Francis said, with his sad, unkind, mocking smile: 'I thought you once said you could pick anyone up . . . ?'

'Well, a girl's a girl, of course. But   '

'Oh, all right, all right,' said Francis. 'Don't think any more of it. Sorry I ever spoke. I detest asking people to do things . . .' Perversely, he reached across for *Esquire*, and Geoff knew one would not see it again. He said to himself that really there were limits. At the same time, he knew the matter would not be dropped; Francis never forgot anything he had set his heart on.

Being crippled made him a difficult child. But what a tough time he had, what a tough time, really. This was the first thing he'd asked for that he had really wanted. It did seem a shame; it did seem rather a shame . . . Geoff stretched and stood up against the sun lounge window. He looked thoughtfully at Tibbie walking away.

Tibbie knew it was odd, but she could not see any harm. She would, naturally, not speak of this to her aunt – this really whirlwind invitation to tea.

For, the following morning, which was even wetter, Geoff had picked Tibbie up, in the Tudor Café, where she sat listlessly drinking her morning coffee, listening to wireless music, looking out at the sea. Geoff picked her up with an ease combined with faultless propriety that left them both decidedly gratified. He had come across to her table – she had taken her hood off and her curls were pressed flat to her head. He said: 'Have you dropped a glove?' and she, knowing she wore none, said: 'Have you found one?' diffidently raising her lashes. 'Well, not this morning,' Geoff said, with his most disarming smile. 'But the fact is, I've got a message for you.' 'Oh – who from?' 'Someone you don't know yet – unless you know him by sight. He feels he knows you by sight . . . My cousin's a cripple,' Geoff concluded. 'It's pretty dull for him here. It would be ever so nice of you if you'd come to tea. . . .'

So here was Tibbie, at half-past four on a Thursday, going up in the Palace Hotel lift. She wore gloves today and wore her prettiest hat. She was ever so slightly disappointed at being sucked upstairs, away from the band. Geoff had not told her they had a private suite.

This made everything much more dashing, grander –
but was it quite so respectable, having tea upstairs? But
this time next year I shall be in India, she thought.

Into the luxurious small room, with its wide sea view,
Tibbie advanced nose first. Francis ran his chair forward to
meet her. 'I'm sorry I cannot get up,' he said. He nodded
to where Geoff stood by the window and said: 'You've
met my cousin, I think?' On satinwood tables stood
vases of tawny flowers, to match the curtains of apricot
silk. Francis spun round his chair to face a great big
armchair into which Tibbie, hypnotized, found herself
sinking down. Her face was now below his: she found
herself looking up at a boy of about twenty, who was
levelling on her his power of making natural people
unnaturally shy. His eyes were brilliant. A dark lock
fell forward over his forehead; she looked at his over-
sensitive hands on the arms of his chair. Dipping her
face down, Tibbie looked round the parlour under her
lashes that were as soft as moths. 'What lovely flowers,'
she said.

'They're for you – they were the best I could get: the
shops are so rotten here. Oh, but I beg your pardon –
you live here, perhaps?'

'No, only my aunt does. I——'

'Then it doesn't matter,' said Francis. 'Look, do
take your gloves off, your hat – do look as though you
would stay!' So Tibbie pulled her gloves off, lifted her
hat off her curls. Francis stared sharply; he said: 'What's
that ring? Why do you wear that?'

'Oh, my engagement ring,' she said, modestly.
Francis let this little confident statement sink into the
masculine silence of the room. Then he twitched his
head round at Geoff and said: 'Why isn't tea coming?

Ring for tea.' Reaching out, he switched on a table-lamp; the dusk outside looked desolate, dark as ink. Tea came rattling cheerfully in on a little trolley; Geoff brought his engaging presence up to the trolley; Francis invited Tibbie to pour out. She could not help peeping at the under-ledge of the trolley – really, she had never seen such a tea! They were all three of them getting on very nicely when Francis said with his self-torturing smile: 'Where are you going to live when you are married?'

'India,' she smiled. 'Doesn't that seem funny?'

'No. You'll hate it. It's very hot.'

'Oh, come,' Geoff said, 'India sounds quite a lot of fun. I should jump at going out to India myself.' 'Pity you can't,' Francis threw at him, slightingly. But Tibbie, biting into a grape tartlet, fluttered in Geoff's direction a grateful look. Geoff went on: 'Francis never thinks much of anyone's plans, you know.'

Francis stonily said: 'I don't need to plan; I plot. I don't believe in plans.' He jerked back his lock of hair and said, directly, to Tibbie: 'Neither do you.' Which made her send Geoff (not Francis) a little look of surprise. Francis said: 'You don't care if you go to India. . . .'

'Oh, but I do.'

'You may not get there,' said Francis.

Geoff started laughing and flushing. 'Oh, shut up,' he said. 'Shut up. You'll make this girl sorry she came to tea; you'll upset her.'

'Are you upset, Tibbie?' said Francis, lightly. She could not speak; she was laughing – real laughter, not awkward, forbidding laughter like Geoff's. Vibrating gently all over, like a small cat emitting a great purr, she unsteadily folded her tea napkin and put back her plate on the trolley. A flake of pastry still clung to her chin; she curved forward over her mirth. 'You sound so funny,' she said. 'You seem to think I have no character. It's so funny, when I've only just come to tea. Why, I've got my destiny lines all over my hand. I've had my hand told three times and it always comes out the same – I am to cross the sea and live in a sunny clime.'

'The sun shines almost everywhere except here. You could live in a villa in Italy.'

'Oh, but you see, I don't know anyone there.'

'I'm going to live in a villa in Italy.'

'I thought you said you never made any plans!' crowed Tibbie, contentedly, looking round her at the lamps, the flowers, the apricot curtains that had been softly drawn. 'But, of course, it's different for you,' she said.

'Yes,' said Francis. 'It's different for me.'

Geoff saw Tibbie down in the lift. He went through the white-pillared lounge with her and pushed her gently ahead of him through the revolving door. In the door she turned round to say something, but it was cut off. When they both came out on the steps and stood where the light streamed through the dark, mild rain, he said: 'Shall I see you home?' 'I don't think so, because . . . All right.' She unfurled her umbrella, then turned her profile away to the dark sea. 'I can't sometimes believe I shall be in India,' she said. 'So I couldn't think what to say when your cousin talked about it. But, of course, I believe in my destiny.'

'I hope you didn't think Francis impertinent?'

'Oh, no; things are different for him aren't they? Always stuck there like that. I should have thought he'd have liked a more lively person than me.'

'All the same, we are meeting again, aren't we?'

'Well, he only said, "Don't go." He didn't say to come back. . . .'

Next morning the sun shone; the sea shone like white glass. The promenade glistened; the curve of the bay, the promenade gardens, with their few wet roses, wore the smile of November, pallidly gay. Francis and his chair went down in the lift and were deferentially bumped by the pages down the hotel steps – then he cruised about in the sun, all by himself, looking for an advantageous position. He had sent Geoff off to play golf with a man they had met last night. Francis stopped his chair by a seat on the promenade. He wore a dark red, high-necked sweater, an expensive tweed coat; a camel-hair rug was tucked over his knees. His cheek-bones were stained by a slight flush; he sat looking side-ways out to sea, his whole nervous attention fixed on the promenade. For some time he sat listening for Tibbie's step; then she came round his chair and stood beside him, blinking her eyelashes in the sun.

'Well,' said Francis, 'here is your sunny clime.'

Tibbie looked at the bench and said: 'Where's Geoff gone?'

'Golf,' said Francis, sharply. 'Why?'

'I just wondered,' she said. She dithered, then sat down. She was wearing no gloves again, so when she spread her hands on her lap, palms upward, she could frown down thoughtfully at the lines on them. Francis said: 'Well? Are they different since yesterday?' 'Oh, how could they change; they are me.' 'Did you like coming to tea?'

'Oh, yes. But you made me feel such a silly.'

'Was that why you kept laughing the whole time? . . .

You can write about that in your letter to India, can't you? – "Oh, I went out to tea with a funny boy." Do you write to India often?'

'Well, I do when I can. But so little happens here, there's not much to write about.'

'*About?*' said Francis. 'But you write love letters, don't you?' Tibbie looked quite mystified; Francis continued: 'Have you and that young man got nothing to say?'

'You see, when I used to know him we were not engaged, really. So I don't know what we said. We played tennis most of the time.'

A contraction shook Francis's chair, and made Tibbie turn round. Perplexed she watched something playing over his face: was it pain, or was it light from the sea? He returned to himself and said in a steady voice: 'You wouldn't play tennis at all well.'

'No, but Tom likes me to try . . . Why are you so sharp with me?'

'I didn't sleep last night.'

'Oh, dear, that does seem a pity, when it's such a lovely morning today. How did you know I didn't play tennis well?'

'I know all about you: I knew you before we met. You knew I knew you, Tibbie? What made you so foolish? You're a sweet, dreadful funk, with no backbone at all. How dared you laugh when I asked you to marry me – when I'm like – *this*?' cried Francis, striking his chair.

'Oh, I *didn't* know you meant that. The whole tea was so funny. I didn't know where I was.'

'You never know where you are.'

'I don't understand. Do you really . . . I mean, *do* you . . .'

'Yes, I naturally love you. I want you always by me. Haven't I just told you I didn't sleep? Listen, Tibbie: I don't ask you to love me; all I want is that you should be always there. All those mornings you've walked past and looked up at the window I've wanted to bang the glass and shout: "Stop, you idiot: stay!" I'm sick and spoilt and impossible and I torment everyone, but now you torment me whenever you go away. Yes, I sent Geoff out yesterday morning to pick you up, like I'd send him out for a newspaper or a bunch of flowers. Yes, I thought it could all be as easy as that. But when you'd gone I knew it was terrible. I've always hated people because I've hated their pity. But I love you: you show me how to be kind. . . .'

Francis checked himself, stopped: he reached out a hand to Tibbie, and she uncertainly let her hand fall into his. She sat looking slantwise past him at the sun-painted sea front, the shining, unreal scene. They both seemed to be somewhere else. Then she drew her hand away, nervous. She said: 'You are kind in such a funny way.'

'Because you are always walking away, going. I want you always by me just as you are, not different. I want you in rooms with me. Stay with me all the time!'

'I'd, I'd be afraid, Francis. You sort of eat me up. Besides——'

'There is no besides. I'm all will and you've no will. I know you don't understand. But I could make you so happy. Look how you liked my room, how you liked the flowers. You understand those, perhaps? I'm rich; I could give you all those small, silly things. Oh, I could shelter you, Tibbie. It's *my* life-line that's in your hand.'

'Yes, but you see . . .'

'But what?'

'But you see, I'm going away today . . . ' She said this looking away, and he did not say anything. 'I'm going away; I got the letter this morning. Tom's mother's come to London; I've got to go up to her. You see, Tom's mother has never seen me, and they say I must certainly go to her.'

Francis said, in a voice that seemed to come from a distance: 'All right, all right, then: go, then, go: then come back.'

But Tibbie knitted her forehead. 'But Tom's mother lives right up in Scotland. And, you see, I'm to go back to Scotland with her. They all say I must. They say Tom would like me to. . . .'

'You can't go,' Francis said, in a perfectly dead voice. 'All that's out of the question – don't you understand?'

'No, I don't – *you* told me I didn't.'

'Yes, but *look*!' cried Francis, striking his chair again. 'You can't leave me when I cannot come after you! You don't *want* to leave me, Tibbie, do you? . . . For God's sake, look straight at me: stop drooping your head!'

But she only bent down more; she curled up like an anemone in an unkind wind. At the same time, with a frightened obstinacy, her soft lashes stayed down on her cheek. Then she said in her mild voice, without even a falter: 'But it's all settled, this morning. My aunt's sent the telegrams; she has ordered the taxi. The taxi's coming at three.'

Francis paused for the last time – the unusual hesitation of someone facing the whole of life. He said: 'But you and I cannot have met for nothing.' But she only raised her hands, which were trembling ever so slightly, and looked again at what had been written there. 'I can't change what's all settled,' she said.

'At the same time you can't go.'

'But I can.' Getting up, she looked in surprise at him – surprised to find herself getting up. It was as though wires moved her. As she turned the end of the bench she heard Francis, behind her, give a wrench at his chair. Her thought was: 'He must not come after me – on wheels, on wheels: wheels turn very fast.' She broke into a run. She ran down the promenade, stooping, breathless, not looking back once, not daring to listen. The cold sea flashed alongside of her. She reached the corner; then she lagged slowly, slowly back to her aunt's gate.

When the promenade was quite empty Francis drove his chair, slowly, in the other direction, to the Palace Hotel.

UNWELCOME IDEA

ALONG Dublin bay, on a sunny July morning, the public gardens along the Dalkey tramline look bright as a series of parasols. Chalk-blue sea appears at the ends of the roads of villas turning downhill – but these are still the suburbs, not the seaside. In the distance, floating across the bay, buildings glitter out of the heat-haze on the neck to Howth, and Howth Head looks higher veiled. After inland Ballsbridge, the tram from Dublin speeds up; it zooms through the residential reaches with the gathering steadiness of a launched ship. Its red velvet seating accommodation is seldom crowded – its rival, the quicker bus, lurches ahead of it down the same road.

After Ballsbridge, the ozone smell of the bay sifts more and more through the smell of chimneys and pollen and the July-darkened garden trees as the bay and line converge. Then at a point you see the whole bay open – there are nothing but flats of grass and the sunk railway between the running tram and the still sea. An immense glaring reflection floods through the tram. When high terraces, backs to the tramline, shut out the view again, even their backs have a salted, marine air: their cotton window-blinds are pulled half down, crooked; here and there an inner door left open lets you see a flash of sea through a house. The weathered lions on gate posts ought to be dolphins. Red, low-lying villas have been fitted between earlier terraces, ornate, shabby, glassy hotels, bow-fronted mansions all built in the first place to stand up over spaces of grass. Looks from trams and voices from public gardens invade the old walled lawns with their grottos and weeping willows. Spit-and-polish alternates with decay. But stucco, slate and slate-fronts, blotched Italian pink-wash, dusty windows, lace curtains and dolphin-lions seem to be the eternity of this tram route. Quite soon the modern will sag, chip, fade. Change leaves everything at the same level. Nothing stays bright but mornings.

The tram slides to stops for its not many passengers. The Blackrock bottleneck checks it, then the Dun Laoghaire. These are the shopping centres strung on the line: their animation congests them. Housewives with burnt bare arms out of their cotton dresses mass blinking and talking among the halted traffic, knocking their shopping-bags on each other's thighs. Forgotten Protestant ladies from 'rooms' near the esplanade stand squeezed between the kerb and the shops. A file of booted children threads its way through the crush, a nun at the head like a needle. Children by themselves curl their toes in their plimsoles and suck sweets and disregard everything. The goods stacked in the shops look very static and hot. Out from the tops of the shops on brackets stand a number of clocks. As though wrought up by the clocks the tram-driver smites his bell again and again, till the checked tram noses its way through.

By half-past eleven this morning one tram to Dalkey is not far on its way. All the time it approaches the Ballsbridge stop Mrs. Kearney looks undecided, but when it does pull up she steps aboard because she has seen no bus. In a slither of rather ungirt parcels, including a dress-box, with a magazine held firmly between her teeth, she clutches her way up the stairs to the top. She settles herself on a velvet seat: she is hot. But the doors at each end and the windows are half-open, and as the tram moves air rushes smoothly through. There are only four other people and no man smokes a pipe. Mrs. Kearney has finished wedging her parcels between her hip and the side of the tram and is intending to look at her magazine when she stares hard ahead and shows interest in someone's back. She moves herself and everything three seats up, leans forward and gives a poke at the back. 'Isn't that you?' she says.

Miss Kevin jumps round so wholeheartedly that the brims of the two hats almost clash. 'Why, for goodness' sake! . . . Are you on the tram?' She settled round in her seat with her elbow hooked over the back – it is bare and sharp, with a rubbed joint: she and Mrs. Kearney are of an age, and the age is about thirty-five. They both wear printed dresses that in this weather stick close to their backs; they are enthusiastic, not close friends but as close as they are ever likely to be. They both have high, fresh, pink colouring; Mrs. Kearney could do with a little less weight and Miss Kevin could do with a little more.

They agree they are out early. Miss Kevin has been in town for the July sales but is now due home to let her mother go out. She has parcels with her but they are compact and shiny, having been made up at the counters of shops. 'They all say, buy now. You never know.' She cannot help looking at Mrs. Kearney's parcels, bursting out from their string. 'And aren't you very laden, also,' she says.

'I tell you what I've been doing,' says Mrs. Kearney. 'I've been saying goodbye to my sister Maureen in Ballsbridge, and who knows how long it's to be for! My sister's off to County Cavan this morning with the whole of her family and the maid.'

'For goodness' sake,' says Miss Kevin. 'Has she relatives there?'

'She has, but it's not that. She's evacuating. For the holidays they always go to Tramore, but this year she says she should evacuate.' This brings Mrs. Kearney's parcels into the picture. 'So she asked me to keep a few of her things for her.' She does not add that Maureen has given her these old things, including the month-old magazine.

'Isn't it well for her,' says Miss Kevin politely. 'But won't she find it terribly slow down there?'

'She will, I tell you,' says Mrs. Kearney. 'However, they're all driving down in the car. She's full of it. She says we should all go somewhere where we don't live. It's nothing to her to shift when she has the motor. But the latest thing I hear they say now in the paper is that we'll be shot if we don't stay where we are. They say now we're all to keep off the roads – and there's my sister this morning with her car at the door. Do you think they'll halt her, Miss Kevin?'

'They might,' says Miss Kevin. 'I hear they're very suspicious. I declare, with the instructions changing so quickly it's better to take no notice. You'd be upside down if you tried to follow them all. It's of the first importance to keep calm, they say, and however would we keep calm doing this, then that? Still, we don't get half the instructions they get in England. I should think they'd really pity themselves ... Have you earth in your house, Mrs. Kearney? We have, we have three buckets. The warden's delighted with us: he says we're models. We haven't a refuge, though. Have you one?'

'We have a kind of pump, but I don't know it is much good. And nothing would satisfy Fergus till he turned out the cellar.'

'Well, you're very fashionable!'

'The contents are on the lawn, and the lawn's ruined. He's crazy,' she says glumly, 'with A.R.P.'

'Aren't men very thorough,' says Miss Kevin with a virgin detachment that is rather annoying. She has kept thumbing her sales parcels, and now she cannot resist undoing one. 'Listen,' she says, 'isn't this a pretty delaine?' She runs the end of a fold between her finger and thumb. 'It drapes sweetly. I've enough for a dress and a bolero. It's French: they say we won't get any more now.'

'And that Coty scent — isn't that French?'

Their faces flood with the glare struck from the sea as the tram zooms smoothly along the open reach — wall and trees on its inland side, grass and bay on the other. The tips of their shingles and the thoughts in their heads are for the minute blown about and refreshed. Mrs. Kearney flutters in the holiday breeze, but Miss Kevin is looking inside her purse. Mrs. Kearney thinks she will take the kids to the strand. 'Are you a great swimmer, Miss Kevin?'

'I don't care for it: I've a bad circulation. It's a fright to see me go blue. They say now the sea's full of mines,' she says, with a look at the great, innocent bay.

'Ah, they're tethered; they'd never bump you.'

'I'm not nervous at any time, but I take a terrible chill.'

'My sister Maureen's nervous. At Tramore she'll never approach the water: it's the plage she enjoys. I wonder what will she do if they stop the car – she has all her plate with her in the back with the maid. And her kiddies are very nervous: they'd never stand it. I wish now I'd asked her to send me a telegram. Or should I telegraph her to know did she arrive? . . . Wasn't it you said we had to keep off the roads?'

'That's in the event of invasion, Mrs. Kearney. In the event of not it's correct to evacuate.'

'She's correct all right, then,' says Mrs. Kearney, with a momentary return to gloom. 'And if nothing's up by the finish she'll say she went for the holiday, and I shouldn't wonder if she still went to Tramore. Still, I'm sure I'm greatly relieved to hear what you say . . . Is that your father's opinion?'

Miss Kevin becomes rather pettish. 'Him?' she says, 'oh gracious, I'd never ask him. He has a great contempt for the whole war. My mother and I daren't refer to it – isn't it very mean of him? He does nothing but read the papers and roar away to himself. And will he let my mother or me near him when he has the news on? You'd think,' Miss Kevin says with a clear laugh, 'that the two of us originated the war to spite him: he doesn't seem to blame Hitler at all. He's really very unreasonable when he's not well. We'd a great fight to get in the buckets of earth, and now he makes out they're only there for the cat. And to hear the warden praising us makes him sour. Isn't it very mean to want us out of it all, when they say the whole of the country is drawn together? He doesn't take any pleasure in A.R.P.'

'To tell you the truth I don't either,' says Mrs.

Kearney. 'Isn't it that stopped Horse Show? Wouldn't that take the heart out of you – isn't that a great blow to national life? I never yet missed a Horse Show – Sheila was nearly born there. And isn't that a terrible blow to trade? I haven't the heart to look for a new hat. To my mind this war's getting very monotonous: all the interest of it is confined to a few . . . Did you go to the Red Cross Fête?'

The tram grinds to a halt in Dun Laoghaire Street. Simultaneously Miss Kevin and Mrs. Kearney move up to the window ends of their seats and look closely down on the shop windows and shoppers. Town heat comes off the street in a quiver and begins to pervade the immobile tram. 'I declare to goodness,' exclaims Miss Kevin, 'there's my same delaine! French, indeed! And watch the figure it's on – it would sicken you.'

But with parallel indignation Mrs. Kearney has just noticed a clock. 'Will you look at the time!' she says, plaintively. 'Isn't this an awfully slow tram! There's my morning gone, and not a thing touched at home, from attending evacuations. It's well for her! She expected me on her step by ten – "It's a terrible parting," she says on the p.c. But all she does at the last is to chuck the parcels at me, then keep me running to see had they the luncheon basket and what had they done with her fur coat . . . I'll be off at the next stop, Miss Kevin dear. Will you tell your father and mother I was inquiring for them?' Crimson again at the very notion of moving, she begins to scrape her parcels under her wing. 'Well,' she says, 'I'm off with the *objets d'art*.' The heels of a pair of evening slippers protrude from a gap at the end of the dress box. The tram-driver, by smiting his bell, drowns any remark Miss Kevin could put out: the tram clears the crowd and moves down Dun Laoghaire Street, between high flights of steps, lace curtains, gardens with round beds. 'Bye-bye, now,' says Mrs. Kearney, rising and swaying.

'Bye-bye to you,' said Miss Kevin. 'Happy days to us all.'

Mrs. Kearney, near the top of the stairs, is preparing to bite on the magazine. 'Go on!' she says. 'I'll be seeing you before then.'

OH, MADAM...

O H, madam . . . Oh, *madam*, here you are!
I don't know what you'll say. Look, sit down
just for a minute, madam; I dusted this chair for
you. Yes, the hall's all right really; you don't see so
much at first – only, our beautiful fanlight gone. No,
there's nothing in here to hurt: I swept up the glass.
Oh, *do* sit a minute, madam; you look quite white . . .
This is a shock for you, isn't it! I was in half a mind to
go out and meet you, but I didn't rightly like to leave
everything. Not with the windows gone. They can
see in.

Oh, *I'm* quite all right, madam. I made some tea
this morning . . . Do I? Oh well, that's natural, I suppose.
I'd be quite all right if I wasn't feeling so bad. Well,
you know how I always was – I don't like a cup to go.
And now . . . If you'll only sit still, madam, I'll go and
get you something. I know you don't take tea, not in
the regular way, but it really is wonderful what tea
does for you . . . Sherry? I'll go and try, but I really
don't know – the dining-room door won't – I'm *afraid*,
madam, I'm afraid it's the ceiling in there gone . . . And
as you know, Johnson's got the key to the cellar, and
Johnson went off after the all clear. I said, 'You did
ought to stay till madam's with us.' But he didn't seem
quite himself – he *did* have a bad night, madam, and

you know how men are, nervous . . . I don't know where
– back to his wife's, I daresay: he didn't vouchsafe . . .
The girls? Oh, *they're* quite well, I'm thankful to say.
They were very good through it, really, better than
Johnson. They'll be back for their things, that is, if——
Well, oh *dear*, madam, wait till you see. . . .

No, I'm all *right*, madam, really . . . Do I? Not more
than you do, I'm sure. This *is* a home-coming for you –
after that nice visit. I don't know what to say to you –
your beautiful house! There usen't to be a thing wrong
in it, used there, madam? I took too much pride in it, I
daresay . . . I *know*, madam, the stairs – all plaster. I
took the dustpan and brush to them, but as fast as you
work it keeps flaking down. It's all got in my hair, under
my cap. I caught a sight of myself in Johnson's mirror
and I said to myself, 'Why, madam will think I've turned
white in the night!' . . . Yes, there it goes; watch it. It's
the shock to the house. Like snow? The things you think
of! You *are* brave!

Oh *no*, madam. No, you get through it somehow.
You'd have been wonderful . . . We'd have done what
we could to make you comfortable, madam, but it would
not have been fit for you – not last night. If I said once
I said a dozen times, to the others, 'Well, thank goodness *madam's* not here tonight; thank goodness
madam's away' . . . Yes, we all sat down in our sitting-
room. It *is* a strong basement. It does rock, but not like
the rest of the house . . . It was that one they dropped
in the cinema that did our damage, madam. They say
what went on the cinema weighed a ton. They should
never have put a cinema, not in this neighbourhood.
However – poor thing, it's not there now . . . No, *I*
haven't, madam; I haven't been out this morning. I

only just saw what I saw from the back. And I'm only glad *you* didn't – it would only distress you. I expect your taxi brought you the other way. All I know I heard from the warden. He seemed to consider we'd had quite an escape.

Well, I suppose we did, madam – that's if you come to think of it. They did seem to have quite set their hearts on us. I don't know how many went in the park. When it was not the bangs it was the hums . . . Well, I don't know, really – what *could* we do? As I say, all things come to an end. It would have sickened you, madam, to hear our glass going. Well, you've *seen* the front. No wonder you came in white. Then that ceiling down. I know *I* thought, 'Well, there does go the house!' Of course I ran up at once, but I couldn't do anything . . . The wardens were nice; they were very nice gentlemen. I don't know how they think of it all, I'm sure.

You won't take *anything*, madam? . . . You'll need your fur coat, excuse me, madam, you will. There's the draught right through the house. You don't want to catch cold, not on top of everything . . . No, it's useless; you *can't* move that dining-room door . . . But the house has been wonderful, madam, really – you really have cause to be proud of it. Yes, it's all right here in the little telephone room – that is – well, you can see for your-self . . . What is it – an ashtray, madam? . . . No, I don't wonder, really: I'm sure if I were a smoker – you have to have *something*, don't you, to fall back on? I'll bring the ashtray upstairs with us for the rest of the stumps . . . Yes, madam, I'll follow, madam. As you say, get it over . . . Oh dear, madam, you *are* upset.

You can't help that; you can't but walk in the plaster. I'll have it all off in a day or two.

Airy? Well yes, if you call it that. I'd sooner our
landing window, I must say. You see, what the warden
said happened, the blast passed through. Well, I don't
know, I'm sure: that was what he said. You have to
have names for things, I suppose.

The drawing-room? Oh, *madam* ... Very well ...
There!

I don't know what to say: really ... You know,
madam, I'd rather last night again than have to show
you all this. It's a piece in the Bible, isn't it, where they
say not to set your heart on anything on this earth. But
that's not nature, not when you care for things ...
Haven't you, madam? It's good of you to say so. I
know how I'd have felt if I'd thought there ever *was*
dust in here. It used to sort of sparkle, didn't it, in its
way ... As it is – why, look, madam: just this rub with my
apron and the cabinet starts to come up again, doesn't it?
Like a mirror – look – as though nothing had happened
... If I could get started in here – but what am I talking
about! The windows gone – it doesn't look decent, does
it ... Oh, I *know*, madam, I know: your satin curtains,
madam! Torn and torn, like a maniac been at them.
Well, he *is* a maniac, isn't he? ... Yes, it did look
worse – I swept up a bit in here. But I don't seem to
have any head – I didn't know where to start.

That's right, madam, go on the balcony. You won't
see so much different from there. To look at the park,
you wouldn't hardly believe ... Sun shining ... Well,
it may do good, I suppose. But this doesn't rightly feel
like a day to me ... All that mess there? That was one
of those last night. Yes, it *sounded* near us, all right:
I hadn't properly looked ... Oh dear, madam, did that
give you a turn?

No, I don't know yet, madam; I haven't heard. I didn't care to go asking out on the street. I expect I'd hear in good time, if—— It doesn't do to meet trouble. No, not Kentish Town, madam, Camden Town . . . Well, I have been wondering, naturally. It did pass through my mind that my sister'd telephone me . . . Well, I would like to – just run up there for a minute? That is, if my sister doesn't telephone me. Just run up there for a minute this afternoon? That always has been my home . . . It's very kind of you, madam: I hope so, too. . . .

Little houses aren't strong, madam. You always worry a bit. When I looked out at the back this morning at some of those little houses, where the mews used to be – (no, don't *you* look out that way, madam; you can't do anything; better look at the park) – I thought, 'Well, they're paper, aren't they.' They're not built to stand up. That was the big bomb they got, the cinema bomb . . . Yes, they always seemed to be nice people: the girls and I used to go through that way to shop. Very quiet; you wouldn't know they were there. I don't think this terrace has ever had to complain . . . Didn't you, madam? No, I hardly suppose you did . . . Well, perhaps they were, madam. Let's hope that they were.

That's right madam, turn up your coat collar. The draught comes right through.

What with you being so good about everything, and now I take another look – well, it might be worse, mightn't it! When we just get the windows back in again – why, madam, I'll have the drawing-room fit for you in no time! I'll sheet my furniture till we're thoroughly swept, then take the electro to the upholstery. Because, look, madam, I don't think anything's *stained*

. . . The clock's going: listen – would you believe that? We mustn't go crying after the curtains, must we? . . . Well, I did, first thing this morning: I couldn't *but* cry. It all seemed to come over me all at once. But now *you're* back – such a difference I feel! Hitler can't beat you and me, madam, can he? If I can just get these glaziers – they expect you to whistle. It's not good for a trade to be too much in demand, is it? It makes the working people ever so slow.

No such great hurry? – I don't understand – I – you – why, madam? *Wouldn't* you wish——?

Why no, I suppose not, madam . . . I hadn't thought. You feel you don't really . . . Not after all this.

But you couldn't ever, not this beautiful house! You couldn't ever . . . I know many ladies *are*. I know many ladies feel it is for the best. You can't but notice all those good houses shut. But, madam, this seemed so much your home——

You must excuse me, madam. I had no right – It was the shock, a minute. I should have thought. The whole thing come on so sudden . . . Why yes, madam; I've no doubt that you should. It will be nice for you down at her ladyship's. All that nice quiet country and everything. We should all wish you to be where it's safe, I'm sure . . . You mean, for the duration? . . . *I* see, madam. I am sure you'll only decide what's right. Only . . . this lovely house, madam. We've all cared for it so . . . I *am* a silly: I was upset this morning, but somehow I never saw us not starting again. . . .

I suppose it might, yes. Happen another night. . . .

All the same, I should like, if you didn't object, madam, to stay on here for the month and get things straight. I'd like to leave things as I found them – fancy,

ten years ago! ... That's very good of you, madam, but
it's been my own satisfaction. If it has made any difference I'm only glad ... I daresay I'm funny in ways,
madam, but it's been quite my life here, really it has ...
I *should* prefer that, if it would suit you. I couldn't think
of workmen round in here without me ... I've been
through so much with this place ... In *any* event,
madam, I should rather be here.

Tonight? ... *I* see, madam, I'm sure they'll be glad
to see you. I'm sure you should lose no time, not after
a shock like this.

We should think of your packing, then, shouldn't we?
If we went up now to your room perhaps you'd just show
me what ... Oh, yes, I see. I hadn't properly thought.
Of course you would need to take everything. When it's
for so long, and – Well, good clothes should be where it's
safe.

The plaster's worse on the second flight, I'm afraid.

Yes ... I was really dreading bringing you up here,
madam. But now you won't want to sleep here for
some time. Your luck's not hurt – look; there's not a
mirror got cracked ... It was that old blast got the little
lamp ... I can't picture you, if I may say so, madam,
waking up in the mornings anywhere not here. Oh,
you've travelled, I know, but you have always been
back. Still, nothing goes on for ever, does it ... Your
dresses, madam – I've been over them: not a speck.
There must be some merciful Providence, mustn't
there?

You won't find such good-fitting cupboards, not at her
ladyship's.

Yes, look at the sun out there. Autumn's always the
nicest season just around here, I think.

Excuse me, madam – Madam, it's nothing, really. I – I – I – I'm really not taking on. I daresay I – got a bit of dust in my eye . . . You're too kind – you make me ashamed, really . . . Yes, I daresay it's the lack of sleep . . . The sun out there . . . If you'll excuse me, madam – I'll give my nose a good blow – that clears a thing off . . . Yes, I will try, when I've just run up to my sister's. I'll try a good nap. But to tell you the truth madam, I shan't truly sleep till I've started to get things straight . . . I'm quite myself now, really. Hope I didn't upset you . . . I'll just run up to the boxroom after the trunks and cases – they'll need some brushing, I *should* think. . . .

That really is what I'd rather, if you have no objection. Johnson and the girls will be round tomorrow, and as you won't be here, madam, no doubt you would like me to . . . And I couldn't leave this house empty, the whole night . . . I know, madam; I know that must come in time . . . Lonely? No; no, *I* don't feel lonely. And this never did feel to me a lonely house.

SUMMER NIGHT

As the sun set its light slowly melted the landscape, till everything was made of fire and glass. Released from the glare of noon, the haycocks now seemed to float on the aftergrass: their freshness penetrated the air. In the not far distance hills with woods up their flanks lay in light like hills in another world – it would be a pleasure of heaven to stand up there, where no foot ever seemed to have trodden, on the spaces between the woods soft as powder dusted over with gold. Against those hills, the burning red rambler roses in cottage gardens along the roadside looked earthy – they were too near the eye.

The road was in Ireland. The light, the air from the distance, the air of evening rushed transversely through the open sides of the car. The rims of the hood flapped, the hood's metal frame rattled as the tourer, in great bounds of speed, held the road's darkening magnetic centre streak. The big shabby family car was empty but for its small driver – its emptiness seemed to levitate it – on its back seat a coat slithered about, and a dressing-case bumped against the seat. The driver did not relax her excited touch on the wheel: now and then while she drove she turned one wrist over, to bring the watch worn on it into view, and she gave the mileage marked on the yellow signposts a flying, jealous, half-inadvertent look. She was driving parallel with the sunset: the sun slowly went down on her right hand.

The hills flowed round till they lay ahead. Where the road bent for its upward course through the pass she pulled up and lighted a cigarette. With a snatch she untwisted her turban; she shook her hair free and threw the scarf behind her into the back seat. The draught of the pass combed her hair into coarse strands as the car hummed up in second gear. Behind one brilliantly-outlined crest the sun had now quite gone; on the steeps of bracken, in the electric shadow, each frond stood out and climbing goats turned their heads. The car came up on a lorry, to hang on its tail, impatient, checked by turns of the road. At the first stretch the driver smote her palm on the horn and shot past and shot on ahead again.

The small woman drove with her chin up. Her existence was in her hands on the wheel and in the sole of the foot in which she felt through the sandal, the throbbing pressure of the accelerator. Her face, enlarged by blown-back hair, was as overbearingly blank as the face of a figure-head; her black eyebrows were ruled level, and her eyes, pupils dilated, did little more than reflect the slow burn of daylight along horizons, the luminous shades of the half-dark.

Clear of the pass, approaching the county town, the road widened and straightened between stone walls and burnished, showering beech. The walls broke up into gateways and hoardings and the suburbs began. People in modern building estate gardens let the car in a hurry through their unseeing look. The raised footpaths had margins of grass. White and grey rows of cottages under the pavement level let woodsmoke over their half-doors:

women and old men sat outside the doors on boxes, looking down at their knees; here and there a bird sprang in a cage tacked to a wall. Children chasing balls over the roadway shot whooping right and left of the car. The refreshed town, unfolding streets to its centre, at this hour slowly heightened, cooled; streets and stones threw off a grey-pink glare, sultry lasting ghost of the high noon. In this dayless glare the girls in bright dresses, strolling, looked like colour-photography.

Dark behind all the windows: not a light yet. The in-going perspective looked meaning, noble and wide. But everybody was elsewhere – the polished street was empty but cars packed both the kerbs under the trees. What was going on? The big tourer dribbled, slipped with animal nervousness between the static, locked cars each side of its way. The driver peered left and right with her face narrow, glanced from her wrist-watch to the clock in the tower, sucked her lip, manoeuvred for somewhere to pull in. The A.A. sign of the hotel hung out from under a balcony, over the steps. She edged in to where it said *Do Not Park*.

At the end of the hotel hall one electric light from the bar shone through a high-up panel: its yellow sifted on to the dusty dusk and a moth could be seen on the glass pane. At the door end came in street daylight, to fall weakly on prints on the oiled walls, on the magenta announcement-strip of a cinema, on the mahogany bench near the receptionist's office, on the hatstand with two forgotten hats. The woman who had come breathlessly up the steps felt in her face a wall of indifference. The impetuous click of her heeled sandals on the linoleum brought no one to the receptionist's desk, and the drone of two talkers in the bar behind the glass panel seemed, like the light, to be blotted up, word by word. The little woman attacked the desk with her knuckles. 'Is there nobody there – I say? Is there nobody *there*?'

'I am, I am. Wait now,' said the hotel woman, who came impassively through the door from the bar. She reached up a hand and fumbled the desk light on, and by this with unwondering negligence studied the customer – the childish, blown little woman with wing-like eyebrows and eyes still unfocused after the long road. The hotel woman, bust on the desk, looked down slowly at the bare legs, the crumple-hemmed linen coat. 'Can I do anything for you?' she said, when she had done.

'I want the telephone – want to put through a call!'

'You can of course,' said the unmoved hotel woman. 'Why not?' she added after consideration, handing across the keys of the telephone cabinet. The little woman made a slide for the cabinet: with her mouth to the mouthpiece, like a conspirator, she was urgently putting her number through. She came out then and ordered herself a drink.

'Is it long distance?'

'Mm-mm . . . What's on here? What are all those cars?'

'Oh, this evening's the dog racing.'

'Is it?'

'Yes, it's the dog racing. We'd a crowd in here, but they're all gone on now.'

'I wondered who they were,' said the little woman, her eyes on the cabinet, sippeting at her drink.

'Yes, they're at the dog racing. There's a wonderful crowd. But I wouldn't care for it,' said the hotel woman, fastidiously puckering up her forehead. 'I went the one time, but it didn't fascinate me.'

The other forgot to answer. She turned away with her drink, sat down, put the glass beside her on the mahogany bench and began to chafe the calves of her bare legs as though they were stiff or cold. A man clasping sheets of unfurled newspaper pushed his way with his elbow through the door from the bar. 'What it says here,' he said, shaking the paper with both hands 'is identically what I've been telling you.'

'That proves nothing,' said the hotel woman. 'However, let it out of your hand.' She drew the sheets of the paper from him and began to fold them into a wad. Her eyes moved like beetles over a top line. 'That's an awful battle. . . .'

'What battle?' exclaimed the little woman, stopping rubbing her legs but not looking up.

'An awful air battle. Destroying each other,' the woman added, with a stern and yet voluptuous sigh. 'Listen, would you like to wait in the lounge?'

'She'd be better there,' put in the man who had brought the paper. 'Better accommodation.' His eyes watered slightly in the electric light. The little woman, sitting upright abruptly, looked defiantly, as though for the first time, at the two watching her from the desk. 'Mr. Donovan has great opinions,' said the hotel woman. 'Will you move yourself out of here?' she asked Mr. Donovan. 'This is very confined – *There's* your call, now!'

But the stranger had packed herself into the telephone box like a conjuror's lady preparing to disappear. '*Hullo?*' she was saying. 'Hullo! I want to speak to——'

'—— You are,' the other voice cut in. 'All right? Anything wrong?'

Her face flushed all over. 'You sound nearer already! I've got to C——.'

The easy, calm voice said: 'Then you're coming along well.'

'Glad, are you?' she said, in a quiver.

'Don't take it too fast,' he said. 'It's a treacherous light. Be easy, there's a good girl.'

'You're a fine impatient man.' His end of the line was silent. She went on: 'I might stay here and go to the dog racing.'

'Oh, is that tonight?' He went on to say equably (having stopped, as she saw it, and shaken the ash off the tip of his cigarette), 'No, I shouldn't do that.'

'Darling. . . .'

'Emma . . . How is the Major?'

'He's all right,' she said, rather defensively.

'I see,' he said. 'Everything quite O.K.?'

'In an hour, I'll be . . . where you live.'

'First gate on the left. Don't kill yourself, there's a good girl. Nothing's worth that. Remember we've got the night. By the way, where are you talking?'

'From the hotel.' She nursed the receiver up close to her face and made a sound into it. Cutting that off she said: 'Well, I'll hang up. I just. . .'

'Right,' he said – and hung up.

Robinson, having hung up the receiver, walked back from the hall to the living-room where his two guests were. He still wore a smile. The deaf woman at the table by the window was pouring herself out another cup of tea. 'That will be very cold!' Robinson shouted – but she only replaced the cosy with a mysterious smile. 'Let her be,' said her brother. 'Let her alone!'

The room in this uphill house was still light: through the open window came in a smell of stocks from the flower beds in the lawn. The only darkness lay in a belt of beech trees at the other side of the main road. From the grate, from the coal of an unlit fire came the fume of a cigarette burning itself out. Robinson still could not help smiling: he reclaimed his glass from the mantelpiece and slumped back with it into his leather armchair in one of his loose, heavy, good-natured attitudes. But Justin Cavey, in the armchair opposite, still looked crucified at having the talk torn. 'Beastly,' he said, 'you've a beastly telephone.' Though he was in Robinson's house for the first time, his sense of attraction to people was marked, early, by just this intransigence and this fretfulness.

'It is and it's not,' said Robinson. That was that. 'Where had we got to?' he amiably asked.

The deaf woman, turning round from the window, gave the two men, or gave the air between them, a penetrating smile. Her brother, with a sort of lurch at his pocket, pulled out a new packet of cigarettes: ignoring Robinson's held-out cigarette case he frowned and split the cellophane with his thumbnail. But, as though his sister had put a hand on his shoulder, his tension could be almost seen to relax. The impersonal, patient look of the thinker appeared in his eyes, behind the spectacles. Justin was a city man, a black-coat, down here (where his sister lived) on holiday. Other summer holidays before this he had travelled in France, Germany, Italy: he disliked the chaotic 'scenery' of his own land. He was down here with Queenie this summer only because of the war, which had locked him in: duty seemed to him better than failed pleasure. His father had been a doctor in this place; now his sister lived on in two rooms in the square – for fear Justin should not be comfortable she had taken a room for him at the hotel. His holiday with his sister, his holiday in this underwater, weedy region of memory, his holiday on which, almost every day, he had to pass the doors of their old home, threatened Justin with a pressure he could not bear. He had to share with Queenie, as he shared the dolls' house meals cooked on the oil stove behind her sitting-room screen, the solitary and almost fairylike world created by her deafness. Her deafness broke down his only defence, talk. He was exposed to the odd, immune, plumbing looks she was for ever passing over his face. He could not deflect the tilted blue of her eyes. The things she said out of nowhere, things with no surface context, were never quite off the mark. She was not all solicitude; she loved to be teasing him.

In her middle-age Queenie was very pretty: her pointed face had the colouring of an imperceptibly fading pink-and-white sweet-pea. This hot summer her artless dresses, with their little lace collars, were mottled over with flowers, mauve and blue. Up the glaring main street she carried a *poult-de-soie* parasol. Her rather dark first-floor rooms faced north, over the square with its grass and lime trees: the crests of great mountains showed above the opposite façades. She would slip in and out on her own errands, as calm as a cat, and Justin, waiting for her at one of her windows, would see her cross the square in the noon sunshine with hands laced over her forehead into a sort of porch. The little town, though strung on a through road, was an outpost under the mountains: in its quick-talking, bitter society she enjoyed, to a degree that surprised Justin, her privileged place. She was woman enough to like to take the man Justin round with her and display him; they went out to afternoon or to evening tea, and in those drawing-rooms of tinted lace and intently-staring family photographs, among octagonal tables and painted cushions, Queenie, with her cotton gloves in her lap, well knew how to contribute, while Justin talked, her airy, brilliant, secretive smiling and looking on. For his part, he was man enough to respond to being shown off – besides, he was eased by these breaks in their *tête-à-tête*. Above all, he was glad, for these hours or two of chatter, not to have to face the screen of his own mind, on which the distortion of every one of his images, the war-broken towers of Europe, constantly stood. The immolation of what had been his own intensely had been made, he could only feel, without any choice of his. In the heart of the neutral Irishman indirect suffering pulled like a crooked knife. So he acquiesced to, and devoured, society: among the doctors, the solicitors, the auctioneers, the bank people of this little town he renewed old acquaintanceships and developed new. He was content to bloom, for this settled number of weeks – so unlike was this to his monkish life in the city – in a sort of tenebrous popularity. He attempted to check his solitary arrogance. His celibacy and his studentish manner could still, although he was past forty, make him acceptable as a young man. In the mornings he read late in his hotel bed; he got up to take his solitary walks; he returned to flick at his black shoes with Queenie's duster and set off with Queenie on their tea-table rounds. They had been introduced to Robinson, factory manager, in the hall of the house of the secretary of the tennis club.

Robinson did not frequent drawing-rooms. He had come here only three years ago, and had at first been taken to be a bachelor – he was a married man living apart from his wife. The resentment occasioned by this discovery had been aggravated by Robinson's not noticing it: he worked at very high pressure in his factory office, and in his off times his high-powered car was to be seen streaking too gaily out of the town. When he was met, his imperturbable male personality stood out to the women unpleasingly, and stood out most of all in that married society in which women aspire to break the male in a man. Husbands slipped him in for a drink when they were alone, or shut themselves up with him in the dining-room. Justin had already sighted him in the hotel bar. When Robinson showed up, late, at the tennis club, his manner with women was easy and teasing, but abstract and perfectly automatic. From this had probably come the legend that he liked women 'only in one way'. From the first time Justin encountered Robinson, he had felt a sort of anxious, disturbed attraction to the big, fair, smiling, offhand, cold-minded man. He felt impelled by Robinson's unmoved physical presence into all sorts of aberrations of talk and mind; he committed, like someone waving an anxious flag, all sorts of absurdities, as though this type of creature had been a woman; his talk became exaggeratedly cerebral, and he became prone, like a perverse person in love, to expose all his own piques, crotchets and weaknesses. One night in the hotel bar with Robinson he had talked until he burst into tears. Robinson had on him the touch of some foreign sun. The acquaintanceship – it could not be called more – was no more than an accident of this narrowed summer. For Justin it had taken the place of travel. The two men were so far off each other's beat that in a city they would certainly not have met.

Asked to drop in some evening or any evening, the

Caveys had tonight taken Robinson at his word. Tonight, the night of the first visit, Justin's high, rather bleak forehead had flushed from the moment he rang the bell. With Queenie behind his shoulder, in muslin, he had flinched confronting the housekeeper. Queenie, like the rest of the town ladies, had done no more till now than go by Robinson's gate.

For her part, Queenie showed herself happy to penetrate into what she had called 'the china house'. On its knoll over the main road, just outside the town, Bellevue did look like china up on a mantelpiece – it was a compact, stucco house with mouldings, recently painted a light blue. From the lawn set with pampas and crescent-shaped flower-beds the hum of Robinson's motor mower passed in summer over the sleepy town. And when winter denuded the trees round them the polished windows, glass porch and empty conservatory sent out, on mornings of frosty sunshine, a rather mischievous and uncaring flash. The almost sensuous cleanness of his dwelling was reproduced in the person of Robinson – about his ears, jaw, collar and close-clipped nails. The approach the Caveys had walked up showed the broad, decided tyre-prints of his car.

'Where had we got to?' Robinson said again.

'I was saying we should have to find a new form.'

'Of course you were,' agreed Robinson. 'That was it.' He nodded over the top of Justin's head.

'A new form for thinking and feeling. . . .'

'But one thinks what one happens to think, or feels what one happens to feel. That is as just so happens – I I should have thought. One either does or one doesn't?'

'One doesn't!' cried Justin. 'That's what I've been getting at. For some time we have neither thought nor

felt. Our faculties have slowed down without our knowing – they had stopped without our knowing! We know
now. Now that there's enough death to challenge
being alive we're facing it that, anyhow, we don't live.
We're confronted by the impossibility *of* living – unless
we can break through to something else. There's been
a stop in our senses and in our faculties that's made
everything round us so much dead matter – and dead
matter we couldn't even displace. We can no longer
express ourselves: what we say doesn't even approximate
to reality; it only approximates to what's been said. I
say, this war's an awful illumination; it's destroyed our
dark; we have to see where we are. Immobilized, God
help us, and each so far apart that we can't even try to
signal each other. And our currency's worthless – our
"ideas", so on, so on. We've got to mint a new one. We've
got to break through to the new form – it needs genius.
We're precipitated, this moment, between genius and
death. I tell you, we must have genius to live at all.'

'I am certainly dished, then,' said Robinson. He got
up and looked for Justin's empty glass and took it to
the sideboard where the decanters were.

'We have it!' cried Justin, smiting the arm of his
chair. 'I salute your genius, Robinson, but I mistrust
my own.'

'That's very nice of you,' said Robinson. 'I agree
with you that this war makes one think. I was in the last,
but I don't remember thinking: I suppose possibly one
had no time. Of course, these days in business one comes
up against this war the whole way through. And to
tell you the truth,' said Robinson, turning round, 'I do
like my off times to *be* my off times, because with this
and then that they are precious few. So I don't really

think as much as I might – though I see how one might always begin. You don't think thinking gets one a bit rattled?'

'I don't think!' said Justin violently.

'Well, you should know,' said Robinson, looking at his thumbnail. 'I should have thought you did. From the way you talk.'

'I couldn't think if I wanted: I've lost my motivation. I taste the dust in the street and I smell the limes in the square and I beat round inside this beastly shell of the past among images that all the more torment me as they lose any sense that they had. As for feeling——'

'You don't think you find it a bit slow here? Mind you, I haven't a word against this place but it's not a place I'd choose for an off time——'

'——My dear Robinson,' Justin said, in a mincing, schoolmasterish tone, 'you seem blind to our exquisite sociabilities.'

'Pack of old cats,' said Robinson amiably.

'You suggest I should get away for a bit of fun?'

'Well, I did mean that.'

'I find my own fun,' said Justin, 'I'm torn, here, by every single pang of annihilation. But that's what I look for; that's what I want completed; that's the whole of what I want to embrace. On the far side of the nothing – my new form. Scrap "me"; scrap my wretched identity and you'll bring to the open some bud of life. I *not* "I" – I'd be the world . . . You're right: what you would call thinking does get me rattled. I only what you call think to excite myself. Take myself away, and I'd *think*. I might see; I might feel purely; I might even love——'

'Fine,' agreed Robinson, not quite easy. He paused

and seemed to regard what Justin had just said – at the same time, he threw a glance of perceptible calculation at the electric clock on the mantelpiece. Justin halted and said: 'You give me too much to drink.'

'You feel this war may improve us?' said Robinson.

'What's love like?' Justin said suddenly.

Robinson paused for just less than a second in the act of lighting a cigarette. He uttered a shortish, temporizing and, for him, unnaturally loud laugh.

Queenie felt the vibration and turned round, withdrawing her arm from the windowsill. She had been looking intently, between the clumps of pampas, down the lawn to the road: cyclists and walkers on their way into town kept passing Robinson's open gate. Across the road, above the demesne wall, the dark beeches let through glitters of sky, and the colour and scent of the mown lawn and the flowers seemed, by some increase of evening, lifted up to the senses as though a new current flowed underneath. Queenie saw with joy in her own mind what she could not from her place in the window see – the blue china house, with all its reflecting windows, perched on its knoll in the brilliant, fading air. They are too rare – visions of where we are.

When the shock of the laugh made her turn round, she still saw day in Robinson's picture-frames and on the chromium fingers of the clock. She looked at Robinson's head, dropped back after the laugh on the leather scroll of his chair: her eyes went from him to Justin. 'Did you two not hit it off?'

Robinson laughed again, this time much more naturally: he emitted a sound like that from inside a furnace in which something is being consumed. Letting his head fall sideways towards Queenie, he seemed to

invite her into his mood. 'The way things come out is
sometimes funny,' he said to Justin, 'if you know what I
mean.'

'No, I don't,' Justin said stonily.

'I bet your sister does.'

'You didn't know what I meant. Anything I may have
said about your genius I do absolutely retract.'

'Look here, I'm sorry,' Robinson said, 'I probably took
you up all wrong.'

'On the contrary: the mistake was mine.'

'You know, it's funny about your sister: I never can
realize she can't hear. She seems so much one of the
party. Would she be fond of children?'

'You mean, why did she not marry?'

'Good God, no – I only had an idea . . .'

Justin went on: 'There was some fellow once, but I
never heard more of him. You'd have to be very on-
coming, I daresay, to make any way with a deaf girl.'

'No, I meant my children,' said Robinson. He had
got up, and he took from his mantelpiece two of the
photographs in silver frames. With these he walked
down the room to Queenie, who received them with her
usual eagerness and immediately turned with them to
the light. Justin saw his sister's profile bent forward in
study and saw Robinson standing above her leaning
against the window frame. When Robinson met an
upward look from Queenie he nodded and touched himself on the chest. 'I can see that – aren't they very like
you?' she said. He pointed to one picture then held up
ten fingers, then to the other and held up eight. 'The
fair little fellow's more like you, the bold one. The dark
one has more the look of a girl – but he will grow up
manly, I daresay . . .' With this she went back to the

photographs: she did not seem anxious to give them up, and Robinson made no movement to take them from her – with Queenie the act of looking was always reflective and slow. To Justin the two silhouettes against the window looked wedded and welded by the dark. 'They are both against me,' Justin thought. 'She does not hear with her ears, he does not hear with his mind. No wonder they can communicate.'

'It's a wonder,' she said, 'that you have no little girl.'

Robinson went back for another photograph – but, standing still with a doubtful look at Queenie, he passed his hand, as though sadly expunging something, back-wards and forwards across the glass. 'She's quite right; we did have a girl,' he said. 'But I don't know how to tell her the kid's dead.'

Sixty miles away, the Major was making his last round through the orchards before shutting up the house. By this time the bronze-green orchard dusk was intense; the clumped curves of the fruit were hardly to be dis-tinguished among the leaves. The brilliance of evening, in which he had watched Emma driving away, was now gone from the sky. Now and then in the grass his foot knocked a dropped apple – he would sigh, stoop rather stiffly, pick up the apple, examine it with the pad of his thumb for bruises and slip it, tenderly as though it had been an egg, into a baggy pocket of his tweed coat. This was not a good apple year. There was something standardized, uncomplaining about the Major's move-ments – you saw a tall, unmilitary-looking man with a stoop and a thinnish, drooping moustache. He often wore a slight frown, of doubt or preoccupation. This frown had intensified in the last months.

As he approached the house he heard the wireless talking, and saw one lamp at the distant end of the drawing-room where his aunt sat. At once, the picture broke up – she started, switched off the wireless and ran down the room to the window. You might have thought the room had burst into flames. 'Quick!' she cried. 'Oh, gracious, quick! – I believe it's the telephone.'

The telephone was at the other side of the house – before he got there he heard the bell ringing. He put his hands in his pockets to keep the apples from bumping as he legged it rapidly down the corridor. When he unhooked on his wife's voice he could not help saying haggardly: 'You all right?'

'Of course. I just thought I'd say good night.'

'That was nice of you,' he said, puzzled. 'How is the car running?'

'Like a bird,' she said in a singing voice. 'How are you all?'

'Well, I was just coming in; Aunt Fran's in the drawing-room listening to something on the wireless, and I made the children turn in half an hour ago.'

'You'll go up to them?'

'Yes, I was just going.' For a moment they both paused on the line, then he said: 'Where have you got to now?'

'I'm at T—— now, at the hotel in the square.'

'At T——? Aren't you taking it rather fast?'

'It's a lovely night; it's an empty road.'

'Don't be too hard on the car, she——'

'Oh, I know,' she said, in the singing voice again. 'At C—— I did try to stop, but there was a terrible crowd there: dog racing. So I came on. Darling . . . ?'

'Yes?'

'It's a lovely night, isn't it?'

'Yes, I was really quite sorry to come in. I shall shut up the house now, then go up to the children; then I expect I'll have a word or two with Aunt Fran.'

'I see. Well, I'd better be pushing on.'

'They'll be sitting up for you, won't they?'

'Surely,' said Emma quickly.

'Thank you for ringing up, dear: it was thoughtful of you.'

'I was thinking about you.'

He did not seem to hear this. 'Well, take care of yourself. Have a nice time.'

'Good night,' she said. But the Major had hung up.

In the drawing-room Aunt Fran had not gone back to the wireless. Beside the evening fire lit for her age, she sat rigid, face turned to the door, plucking round and round the rings on her left hand. She wore a foulard dress, net jabot and boned-up collar, of the type ladies wear to dine in private hotels. In the lamplight her waxy features appeared blurred, even effaced. The drawing-room held a crowd of chintz-covered chairs, inlaid tables and wool-worked stools; very little in it was antique, but nothing was strikingly up-to-date. There were cabinets of not rare china, and more blue-and-white plates, in metal clamps, hung in lines up the walls between water-colours. A vase of pink roses arranged by the governess already dropped petals on the piano. In one corner stood a harp with two broken strings – when a door slammed or one made a sudden movement this harp gave out a faint vibration or twang. The silence for miles around this obscure country house seemed to gather inside the folds of the curtains and to dilute the indoor air like a mist. This room Emma liked too little to touch already felt the touch of decay; it threw lifeless reflections into the two mirrors – the walls were green. Aunt Fran's body was stranded here like some object on the bed of a pool that has run dry. The magazine that she had been looking at had slipped from her lap to the black fur rug.

As her nephew appeared in the drawing-room door Aunt Fran fixed him urgently with her eyes. '*Nothing wrong?*'

'No, no – that was Emma.'

'What's happened?'

'Nothing. She rang up to say good night.'

'But she had said good night,' said Aunt Fran in her troubled way. 'She said good night to us when she was in the car. You remember, it was nearly night when she left. It seemed late to be starting to go so far. She had the whole afternoon, but she kept putting off, putting off. She seemed to me undecided up to the very last.'

The Major turned his back on his aunt and began to unload his pockets, carefully placing the apples, two by two, in a row along the chiffonier. 'Still, it's nice for her having this trip,' he said.

'There was a time in the afternoon,' said Aunt Fran, 'when I thought she was going to change her mind. However, she's there now – did you say?'

'Almost,' he said, 'not quite. Will you be all right if I go and shut up the house? And I said I would look in on the girls.'

'Suppose the telephone rings?'

'I don't think it will, again. The exchange will be closing, for one thing.'

'This afternoon,' said Aunt Fran, 'it rang four times.'

She heard him going from room to room, unfolding

and barring the heavy shutters and barring and chaining the front door. She could begin to feel calmer now that the house was a fortress against the wakeful night. 'Hi!' she called, 'don't forget the window in here' — looking back over her shoulder into the muslin curtains that seemed to crepitate with dark air. So he came back, with his flat, unexpectant step. 'I'm not cold,' she said, 'but I don't like dark coming in.'

He shuttered the window. 'I'll be down in a minute.'

'Then we might sit together?'

'Yes, Aunt Fran: certainly.'

The children, who had been talking, dropped their voices when they heard their father's step on the stairs. Their two beds creaked as they straightened themselves and lay silent, in social, expectant attitudes. Their room smelled of toothpaste; the white presses blotted slowly into the white walls. The window was open, the blind up, so in here darkness was incomplete — obscured, the sepia picture of the Good Shepherd hung over the mantelpiece. 'It's all right,' they said, 'we are quite awake.' So the Major came round and halted between the two beds. 'Sit on mine,' said Di nonchalantly. 'It's my turn to have a person tonight.'

'Why did Mother ring up?' said Vivie, scrambling up on her pillow.

'Now how on earth did *you* know?'

'We knew by your voice — we couldn't hear what you said. We were only at the top of the stairs. Why did she?'

'To tell me to tell you to be good.'

'She's said that,' said Vivie, impatient. 'What did she say truly?'

'Just good night.'

'Oh. Is she there?'

'Where?'

'Where she said she was going to.'

'Not quite – nearly.'

'Goodness!' Di said; 'it seems years since she went.' The two children lay cryptic and still. Then Di went on: 'Do you know what Aunt Fran said because Mother went away without any stockings?'

'No,' said the Major, 'and never mind.'

'Oh, *I* don't mind,' Di said, 'I just heard.' 'And I heard,' said Vivie: she could be felt opening her eyes wide, and the Major could just see, on the pillow, an implacable miniature of his wife's face. Di went on: 'She's so frightened something will happen.'

'Aunt Fran is?'

'She's always frightened of that.'

'She is very fond of us all.'

'Oh,' burst out Vivie, 'but Mother likes things to happen. She was whistling all the time she was packing up. Can't *we* have a treat tomorrow?'

'Mother'll be back tomorrow.'

'But *can't* we have a treat?'

'We'll see; we'll ask Mother,' the Major said.

'Oh yes, but suppose she didn't come back?'

'Look, it's high time you two went to sleep.'

'We can't: we've got all sorts of ideas ... *You* say something, Daddy. Tell us something. Invent.'

'Say what?' said the Major.

'Oh goodness,' Vivie said; '*something*. What do you say to Mother?'

He went downstairs to Aunt Fran with their dissatisfied kisses stamped on his cheek. When he had gone

Di fanned herself with the top of her sheet. 'What makes him so disappointed, do you know?'

'I know, he thinks about the war.'

But it was Di who, after the one question, unlocked all over and dropped plumb asleep. It was Vivie who, turning over and over, watched in the sky behind the cross of the window the tingling particles of the white dark, who heard the moth between the two window-sashes, who fancied she heard apples drop in the grass. One arbitrary line only divided this child from the animal: all her senses stood up, wanting to run the night. She swung her legs out of bed and pressed the soles of her feet on the cool floor. She got right up and stepped out of her nightdress and set out to walk the house in her skin. From each room she went into the human order seemed to have lapsed – discovered by sudden light, the chairs and tables seemed set round for a mouse's party on a gigantic scale. She stood for some time outside the drawing-room door and heard the unliving voices of the Major and aunt. She looked through the ajar door to the kitchen and saw a picked bone and a teapot upon the table and a maid lumped mute in a man's arms. She attempted the front door, but did not dare to touch the chain: she could not get out of the house. She returned to the schoolroom, drawing her brows together, and straddled the rocking-horse they had not ridden for years. The furious bumping of the rockers woke the canaries under their cover: they set up a wiry springing in their cage. She dismounted, got out the box of chalks and began to tattoo her chest, belly and thighs with stars and snakes, red, yellow and blue. Then, taking the box of chalks with her, she went to her mother's room for a look in the long glass – in front of this she attempted to tattoo her behind. After this she bent right down and squinted, upside down between her legs, at the bedroom – the electric light over the dressing-table poured into the vacantly upturned mirror and on to Emma's left-behind silver things. The anarchy she felt all through the house tonight made her, when she had danced in front of the long glass, climb up to dance on the big bed. The springs bounced her higher and higher; chalk-dust flew from her body on to the fleece of the blankets, on to the two cold pillows that she was trampling out of their place. The bed-castors lunged, under her springing, over the threadbare pink bridal carpet of Emma's room.

Attacked by the castors, the chandelier in the drawing-room tinkled sharply over Aunt Fran's head.

She at once raised her eyes to the ceiling. 'Something has got in,' she said calmly – and, rising, made for the drawing-room door. By reflex, the Major rose to stop her: he sighed and put his weak whisky down. 'Never mind,' he said, 'Aunt Fran. It's probably nothing. I'll go.'

Whereupon, his Aunt Fran wheeled round on him with her elbows up like a bird's wings. Her wax features sprang into stony prominence. 'It's never me, never me, never me! Whatever *I* see, whatever I hear it's "nothing", though the house might fall down. You keep everything back from me. No one speaks the truth to me but the man on the wireless. Always things being said on the telephone, always things being moved about, always Emma off at the end of the house singing, always the children hiding away. I am never told, never told, never told. I get the one answer, "nothing". I am expected to wait here. No one comes near the drawing-room. I am never allowed to go and see!'

'If's that's how you feel,' he said, 'do certainly go.'
He thought: it's all right, I locked the house.

So it was Aunt Fran's face, with the forehead lowered,
that came by inches round Emma's door. She appeared
to present her forehead as a sort of a buffer, obliquely
looked from below it, did not speak. Her glance, arriving
gradually at its object, took in the child and the whole
room. Vivie paused on the bed, transfixed, breathless,
her legs apart. Her heart thumped; her ears drummed;
her cheeks burned. To break up the canny and com-
prehensive silence she said loudly: 'I am all over snakes.'

'So this is what . . .' Aunt Fran said. 'So this is
what . . .'

'I'll get off this bed, if you don't like.'

'The bed you were born in,' said Aunt Fran.

Vivie did not know what to do; she jumped off the
bed saying: 'No one told me not to.'

'Do you not know what is wicked?' said Aunt Fran —
but with no more than estranged curiosity. She
approached and began to try to straighten the bed, her
unused hands making useless passes over the surface,
brushing chalk-dust deeper into the fleece. All of a
sudden, Vivie appeared to feel some majestic effluence
from her aunt's person: she lagged round the bed to
look at the stooping, set face, at the mouth held in a
curve like a dead smile, at the veins in the downcast
eyelids and the backs of the hands. Aunt Fran did not
hurry her ceremonial fumbling; she seemed to exalt the
moment that was so fully hers. She picked a pillow up
by its frill and placed it high on the bolster.

'That's mother's pillow,' said Vivie.

'Did you say your prayers tonight?'

'Oh, *yes*.'

'They didn't defend you. Better say them again. Kneel down and say to Our Lord——'

'In my skin?'

Aunt Fran looked directly at, then away from, Vivie's body, as though for the first time. She drew the eiderdown from the foot of the bed and made a half-blind sweep at Vivie with it, saying: 'Wrap up, wrap up.' 'Oh, they'll come off – my snakes!' said Vivie, backing away. But Aunt Fran, as though the child were on fire, put into motion an extraordinary strength – she rolled, pressed and pounded Vivie up in the eiderdown until only the prisoner's dark eyes, so like her mother's, were left free to move wildly outside the great sausage, of padded taffeta, pink.

Aunt Fran, embracing the sausage firmly, repeated: 'Now say to Our Lord——'

Shutting the door of her own bedroom, Aunt Fran felt her heart beat. The violence of the stranger within her ribs made her sit down on the ottoman – meanwhile, her little clock on the mantelpiece loudly and, it seemed to her, slowly ticked. Her window was shut, but the pressure of night silence made itself felt behind the blind, on the glass.

Round the room, on ledges and brackets, stood the fetishes she travelled through life with They were mementoes – photos in little warped frames, musty, round straw boxes, china kittens, palm crosses, the three Japanese monkeys, *bambini*, a Lincoln Imp, a merry-thought pen-wiper, an ivory spinning-wheel from Cologne. From these objects the original virtue had by now almost evaporated. These gifts' givers, known on her lonely journey, were by now faint as their photographs: she no longer knew, now, where anyone was. All the more, her nature clung to these objects that moved with her slowly towards the dark.

Her room, the room of a person tolerated, by now gave off the familiar smell of herself – the smell of the old. A little book wedged the mirror at the angle she liked. When she was into her ripplecloth dressing-gown she brushed and plaited her hair and took out her teeth. She wound her clock and, with hand still trembling a little, lighted her own candle on the commode, then switched off her nephew's electric light. The room contracted round the crocus of flame as she knelt down slowly beside her bed – but while she said the Lord's Prayer she could not help listening, wondering what kept the Major so long downstairs. She never felt free to pray till she had heard the last door shut, till she could relax her watch on the house. She never could pray until they were *all* prostrate – loaned for at least some hours to innocence, sealed by the darkness over their lids.

Tonight she could not attempt to lift up her heart. She could, however, abase herself, and she abased herself for them all. The evil of the moment down in the drawing-room, the moment when she had cried, 'It is never me!' clung like a smell to her, so closely that she had been eager to get her clothes off, and did not like, even now, to put her hands to her face.

Who shall be their judge? Not I.

The blood of the world is poisoned, feels Aunt Fran, with her forehead over the eiderdown. Not a pure drop comes out at any prick – yes, even the heroes shed black blood. The solitary watcher retreats step by step from his post – who shall stem the black tide coming in? There are no more children: the children are born knowing. The shadow rises up the cathedral tower, up the side of the pure hill. There is not even the past: our memories share with us the infected zone; not a memory does not lead up to this. Each moment is everywhere, it holds the war in its crystal; there is no elsewhere, no other place. Not a benediction falls on this apart house of the Major; the enemy is within it, creeping about. Each heart here falls to the enemy.

So this is what goes on. . . .

Emma flying away – and not saying why, or where. And to wrap the burning child up did not put out the fire. You cannot look at the sky without seeing the shadow, the men destroying each other. What is the matter tonight – is there a battle? This is a threatened night.

Aunt Fran sags on her elbows; her knees push desperately in the woolly rug. She cannot even repent; she is capable of no act; she is undone. She gets up and eats a biscuit, and looks at the little painting of Mont Blanc on the little easel beside her clock. She still does not hear the Major come up to bed.

Queenie understood that the third child, the girl, was dead: she gave back the photograph rather quickly, as though unbearable sadness emanated from it. Justin, however, came down the room and looked at the photograph over Robinson's shoulder – at the rather vulgar, frank, blonde little face. He found it hard to believe that a child of Robinson's should have chosen the part of death. He then went back to the table and picked up, with a jerky effrontery, the photographs of the two little boys. 'Do they never come here?' he said. 'You have plenty of room for them.'

'I daresay they will; I mean to fix up something. Just now they're at Greystones,' Robinson said – he then looked quite openly at the clock.

'With their mother?' Justin said, in a harsh impertinent voice.

'Yes, with my wife.'

'So you keep up the two establishments?'

Even Robinson glanced at Justin with some surprise. 'If you call it that,' he said indifferently. 'I rather landed myself with this place, really – as a matter of fact, when I moved in it looked as though things might work out differently. First I stopped where you are, at the hotel, but I do like to have a place of my own. One feels freer, for one thing.'

'There's a lot in that,' said Justin, with an oblique smile. 'Our local ladies think you keep a Bluebeard's castle up here.'

'What, corpses?' Robinson said, surprised.

'Oh yes, they think you're the devil.'

'Who, me?' replied Robinson, busy replacing photographs on the mantelpiece. 'That's really very funny: I'd no idea. I suppose they may think I've been pretty slack – but I'm no good at teafights, as a matter of fact. But I can't see what else can be eating them. What ought I to do, then? Throw a party here? I will if your sister'll come and pour out tea – but I don't think I've really got enough chairs . . . I hope,' he added, looking at Queenie, '*she* doesn't think it's not all above board here?'

'You're forgetting again: she misses the talk, poor girl.'

'She doesn't look very worried.'

'I daresay she's seldom been happier. She's built up

quite a romance about this house. She has a world to herself – I could envy her.'

Robinson contrived to give the impression that he did not wish to have Queenie discussed – partly because he owned her, he understood her, partly because he wished to discuss nothing: it really was time for his guests to go. Though he was back again in his armchair, regard for time appeared in his attitude. Justin could not fail to connect this with the telephone and the smile that had not completely died. It became clear, staringly clear, that throughout the evening his host had been no more than marking time. This made Justin say 'Yes' (in a loud, pertinacious voice), 'this evening's been quite an event for us. Your house has more than its legend, Robinson; it has really remarkable character. However, all good things——' Stiff with anger, he stood up.

'Must you?' said Robinson, rising. 'I'm so sorry.'

Lighting-up time, fixed by Nature, had passed. The deaf woman, from her place in the window, had been watching lights of cars bend over the hill. Turning with the main road, that had passed the foot of the mountains, each car now drove a shaft of extreme brilliance through the dark below Robinson's pampas-grass. Slipping, dropping with a rush past the gate, illuminating the dust on the opposite wall, car after car vanished after its light – there was suddenly quite a gust of them, as though the mountain country, before sleeping, had stood up and shaken them from its folds. The release of movement excited Queenie – that and the beat of light's wings on her face. She turned round very reluctantly as Justin approached and began to make signs to her.

'Why, does Mr. Robinson want us to go?' she said.

'That's the last thing I want!' shouted Robinson. ('She can't hear you.')

'Christ . . .' said Robinson, rattled. He turned the lights on – the three, each with a different face of despair, looked at each other across the exposed room, across the tea-tray on the circular table and the superb leather backs of the chairs. 'My brother thinks we've kept you too long,' she said – and as a lady she looked a little shaken, for the first time unsure of herself. Robinson would not for worlds have had this happen; he strode over and took and nursed her elbow, which tensed then relaxed gently inside the muslin sleeve. He saw, outdoors, his window cast on the pampas, saw the whole appearance of shattered night. She looked for reassurance into his face, and he saw the delicate lines in hers.

'And look how late it's got, Mr. Robinson!'

'It's not that,' he said in his naturally low voice, 'But——'

A car pulled up at the gate. Alarmed by the lit window it cut its lights off and could be felt to crouch there, attentive, docile, cautious, waiting to turn in. 'Your friend is arriving,' Justin said.

On that last lap of her drive, the eighteen miles of flat road along the base of the mountains, the last tingling phase of darkness had settled down. Grassy sharpness passed from the mountains' outline, the patches of firs, the gleam of watery ditch. The west sky had gradually drunk its yellow and the ridged heights that towered over her right hand became immobile cataracts, sensed not seen. Animals rising out of the ditches turned to Emma's headlamps green lamp-eyes. She felt the shudder of

night, the contracting bodies of things. The quick air
sang in her ears; she drove very fast. At the cross-
roads above Robinson's town she pulled round in a wide
swerve: she saw the lemon lights of the town strung along
under the black trees, the pavements and the pale,
humble houses below her in a faint, mysterious glare as
she slipped down the funnel of hill to Robinson's gate.
(The first white gate on the left, you cannot miss it,
he'd said.) From the road she peered up the lawn and
saw, between pampas-tufts, three people upright in his
lit room. So she pulled up and switched her lights and
her engine off and sat crouching in her crouching car
in the dark – night began to creep up her bare legs. Now
the glass porch sprang into prominence like a lantern –
she saw people stiffly saying goodbye. Down the drive
came a man and woman almost in flight; not addressing
each other, not looking back – putting the back of a
fist to her mouth quickly Emma checked the uprush of
an uncertain laugh. She marked a lag in the steps –
turning their heads quickly the man and woman looked
with involuntary straightness into the car, while her
eyes were glued to their silhouettes. The two turned
down to the town and she turned in at the gate.

Farouche, with her tentative little swagger and
childish, pleading air of delinquency, Emma came to a
halt in Robinson's living-room. He had pulled down the
blind. She kept recoiling and blinking and drawing
her fingers over her eyes, till Robinson turned off the
top light. 'Is that that?' There was only the reading-
lamp.

She rested her shoulder below his and grappled their
enlaced fingers closer together as though trying to draw
calmness from him. Standing against him, close up

under his height, she held her head up and began to look round the room. 'You're whistling something,' she said, after a moment or two.

'I only mean, take your time.'

'Why, am I nervous?' she said.

'Darling, you're like a bat in out of the night. I told you not to come along too fast.'

'I see now, I came too early,' she said. 'Why didn't you tell me you had a party? Who were they? What were they doing here?'

'Oh, they're just people in this place. He's a bit screwy and she's deaf, but I like them, as a matter of fact.'

'They're mackintoshy sort of people,' she said. 'But I always thought you lived all alone . . . Is there anyone else in the house now?'

'Not a mouse,' said Robinson, without change of expression. 'My housekeeper's gone off for the night.'

'I see,' said Emma. 'Will you give me a drink?'

She sat down where Justin had just been sitting, and, bending forward with a tremulous frown, began to brush ash from the arm of the chair. You could feel the whole of her hesitate. Robinson, without hesitation, came and sat easily on the arm of the chair from which she had brushed the ash. 'It's sometimes funny,' he said, 'when people drop in like that. "My God," I thought when I saw them, "what an evening to choose." ' He slipped his hand down between the brown velvet cushion and Emma's spine, then spread the broad of his hand against the small of her back. Looking kindly down at her closed eyelids he went on: 'However, it all went off all right. Oh, and there's one thing I'd like to tell you – that chap called me a genius.'

'How would he know?' said Emma, opening her eyes.

'We never got that clear. I was rather out of my depth. His sister was deaf . . .' here Robinson paused, bent down and passed his lips absently over Emma's forehead. 'Or did I tell you that?'

'Yes, you told me that . . . Is it true that this house is blue?'

'You'll see tomorrow.'

'There'll hardly be time, darling; I shall hardly see this house in the daylight. I must go on to – where I'm supposed to be.'

'At any rate, I'm glad that was all O.K. They're not on the telephone, where you're going?'

'No, it's all right; they're not on the telephone . . . *You'll* have to think of something that went wrong with my car.'

'That will all keep,' said Robinson. 'Here you are.'

'Yes, here I am.' She added: 'The night was lovely,' speaking more sadly than she knew. Yes, here she was, being settled down to as calmly as he might settled down to a meal. Her naivety as a lover . . . She could not have said, for instance, how much the authoritative male room – the electric clock, the sideboard, the unlit grate, the cold of the leather chairs – put, at every moment when he did not touch her, a gulf between her and him. She turned her head to the window. 'I smell flowers.'

'Yes, I've got three flower-beds.'

'Darling, for a minute could we go out?'

She moved from his touch and picked up Queenie's tea-tray and asked if she could put it somewhere else. Holding the tray (and given countenance by it) she halted in front of the photographs. 'Oh . . .' she said.

'Yes. Why?' 'I wish in a way you hadn't got any children.' 'I don't see why I shouldn't have: you have.'

'Yes, I . . . But Vivie and Di are not so much *like* children——'

'If they're like you,' he said, 'those two will be having a high old time, with the cat away——'

'Oh darling, I'm not the cat.'

In the kitchen (to put the tray down) she looked round: it shone with tiling and chromium and there seemed to be switches in every place. 'What a whole lot of gadgets you have,' she said. 'Look at all those electric . . .' 'Yes I like them.' 'They must cost a lot of money. My kitchen's all over blacklead and smoke and hooks. My cook would hate a kitchen like this.'

'I always forget that you have a cook.' He picked up an electric torch and they went out. Going along the side of the house, Robinson played a mouse of light on the wall. 'Look, really blue.' But she only looked absently. 'Yes – But have I been wrong to come?' He led her off the gravel on to the lawn, till they reached the edge of a bed of stocks. Then he firmly said: 'That's for you to say, my dear girl.'

'I know it's hardly a question – I hardly know you, do I?'

'We'll be getting to know each other,' said Robinson.

After a minute she let go of his hand and knelt down abruptly beside the flowers: she made movements like scooping the scent up and laving her face in it – he, meanwhile, lighted a cigarette and stood looking down. 'I'm glad you like my garden,' he said. 'You feel like getting fond of the place?'

'You say you forget that I have a cook.'

'Look, sweet, if you can't get that off your mind

you'd better get in your car and go straight home . . . But you will.'

'Aunt Fran's so old, too old; it's not nice. And the Major keeps thinking about the war. And the children don't think I am good; I regret that.'

'You have got a nerve,' he said, 'but I love that. You're with me. Aren't you with me? – Come out of that flower-bed.'

They walked to the brow of the lawn; the soft feather-plumes of the pampas rose up a little over her head as she stood by him overlooking the road. She shivered. 'What are all those trees?' 'The demesne – I know they burnt down the castle years ago. The demesne's great for couples.' 'What's in there?' 'Nothing, I don't think; just the ruin, a lake. . . .'

'I wish——'

'Now, what?'

'I wish we had more time.'

'Yes: we don't want to stay out all night.'

So taught, she smothered the last of her little wishes for consolation. Her shyness of further words between them became extreme; she was becoming frightened of Robinson's stern, experienced delicacy on the subject of love. Her adventure became the quiet practice with him. The adventure (even, the pilgrimage) died at its root, in the childish part of her mind. When he had headed her off the cytherean terrain – the leaf-drowned castle ruin, the lake – she thought for a minute he had broken her heart, and she knew now he had broken her fairytale. He seemed content – having lit a new cigarette – to wait about in his garden for a few minutes longer: not poetry but a sort of tactile wisdom came from the firmness, lawn, under their feet. The white gateposts, the boles of beeches above the dust-whitened wall were just seen in reflected light from the town. There was no moon, but dry, tense, translucent darkness: no dew fell.

Justin went with his sister to her door in the square. Quickly, and in their necessary silence, they crossed the grass under the limes. Here a dark window reflected one of the few lamps, there a shadow crossed a lit blind, and voices of people moving under the trees made a reverberation in the box of the square. Queenie let herself in; Justin heard the heavy front door drag shut slowly across the mat. She had not expected him to come in, and he did not know if she shared his feeling of dissonance, or if she recoiled from shock, or if she were shocked at all. Quitting the square at once, he took the direct way to his hotel in the main street. He went in at the side door, past the bar in which he so often encountered Robinson.

In his small, harsh room he looked first at his bed. He looked, as though out of a pit of sickness, at his stack of books on the mantelpiece. He writhed his head round sharply, threw off his coat and begun to unknot his tie. Meanwhile he beat round, in the hot light, for some crack of outlet from his constriction. It was at his dressing-table, for he had no other, that he began and ended his letter to Robinson: the mirror screwed to the dressing-table constituted a witness to this task – whenever his look charged up it met his own reared head, the flush heightening on the bridge of the nose and forehead, the neck from which as though for an execution, the collar had been taken away.

My dear Robinson: Our departure from your house
(Bellevue, I think?) tonight was so awkwardly late, and
at the last so hurried, that I had inadequate time in
which to thank you for your hospitality to my sister and
to myself. That we exacted this hospitality does not
make its merit, on your part, less. Given the incon-
venience we so clearly caused you, your forbearance with
us was past praise. So much so that (as you may be glad
to hear) my sister does not appear to realize how very
greatly we were *de trop*. In my own case – which is
just – the same cannot be said. I am conscious that, in
spite of her disability, she did at least prove a less weari-
some guest than I.

My speculations and queries must, to your mind,
equally seem absurd. This evening's fiasco has been
definitive: I think it better our acquaintance should close.
You will find it in line with my usual awkwardness that
I should choose to state this decision of mine at all.
Your indifference to the matter I cannot doubt. My
own lack of indifference must make its last weak exhibi-
tion in this letter – in which, if you have fine enough
nostrils (which I doubt) every sentence will almost
certainly stink. In attempting to know you I have
attempted to enter, and to comport myself in, what
might be called an area under your jurisdiction. If my
inefficacies appeared to you ludicrous, my curiosities (as
in one special instance tonight) appeared more – revolting.
I could gauge (even before the postscript outside your
gate) how profoundly I had offended you. Had we either
of us been gentlemen, the incident might have passed off
with less harm.

My attempts to know you I have disposed of already.
My wish that you should know me has been, from the

first, ill found. You showed yourself party to it in no sense, and the trick I played on myself I need not discuss. I acted and spoke (with regard to you) upon assumptions you were not prepared to warrant. You cannot fail to misunderstand what I mean when I say that a year ago this might not have happened to me. But – the assumptions on which I acted, Robinson, are becoming more general in a driven world than you yet (or may ever) know. The extremity to which we are each driven must be the warrant for what we do and say.

My extraordinary divagation towards you might be said to be, I suppose, an accident of this summer. But there are no accidents. I have the fine (yes) fine mind's love of the fine plume, and I meet no fine plumes down my own narrow street. Also, in this place (birthplace) you interposed your solidity between me and what might have been the full effects of an exacerbating return. In fact, you had come to constitute for me a very genuine holiday. As things are, my five remaining days here will have to be seen out. I shall hope not to meet you, but must fear much of the trap-like size of this town. (You need not, as I mean to, avoid the hotel bar.) Should I, however, fail to avoid you, I shall again, I suppose, have to owe much, owe any face I keep, to your never-failing imperviousness. Understand that it will be against my wish that I re-open this one-sided account.

I wish you good night. Delicacy does not deter me from adding that I feel my good wish to be superfluous. I imagine that, incapable of being haunted, you are incapable of being added to. Tomorrow (I understand) you will feel fine, but you will not know any more about love. If the being outside your gate came with a question,

it is possible that she should have come to me. If I had
even seen her she might not go on rending my heart.
As it is, as you are, I perhaps denounce you as much on
her behalf as my own. Not trying to understand, you
at least cannot misunderstand the mood and hour in
which I write. As regards my sister, please do not dis-
continue what has been your even kindness to her: she
might be perplexed. She has nothing to fear, I think.
Accept, my dear Robinson (without irony) my kind
regards,   J.C.

Justin, trembling, smote a stamp on this letter. Going
down as he was, in the hall he unhooked his mackintosh
and put it over his shirt. It was well past midnight;
the street, empty, lay in dusty reaches under the few
lamps. Between the shutters his step raised an echo;
the cold of the mountains had come down; two cats in
his path unclinched and shot off into the dark. On his
way to the letterbox he was walking towards Bellevue;
on his way back he still heard the drunken woman
sobbing against the telegraph pole. The box would not
be cleared till tomorrow noon.

Queenie forgot Justin till next day. The house in
which her rooms were was so familiar that she went
upstairs without a pause in the dark. Crossing her sitting-
room she smelled oil from the cooker behind the screen:
she went through an arch to the cubicle where she slept.
She was happy. Inside her sphere of silence that not a
word clouded, the spectacle of the evening at Bellevue
reigned. Contemplative, wishless, almost without an
'I', she unhooked her muslin dress at the wrists and waist,
stepped from the dress and began to take down her hair.

Still in the dark, with a dreaming sureness of habit, she dropped hairpins into the heart-shaped tray.

This was the night she knew she would find again. It had stayed living under a film of time. On just such a summer night, once only, she had walked with a lover in the demesne. His hand, like Robinson's, had been on her elbow, but she had guided him, not he her, because she had better eyes in the dark. They had gone down walks already deadened with moss, under the weight of July trees; they had felt the then fresh aghast ruin totter above them; there was a moonless sky. Beside the lake they sat down, and while her hand brushed the ferns in the cracks of the stone seat emanations of kindness passed from him to her. The subtle deaf girl had made the transposition of this nothing or everything into an everything – the delicate deaf girl that the man could not speak to and was afraid to touch. She who, then so deeply contented, kept in her senses each frond and breath of that night, never saw him again and had soon forgotten his face. That had been twenty years ago, till tonight when it was now. Tonight it was Robinson who, guided by Queenie down leaf tunnels, took the place on the stone seat by the lake.

The rusted gates of the castle were at the end of the square. Queenie, in her bed facing the window, lay with her face turned sideways, smiling, one hand lightly against her cheek.